T0190906

CRAFTING A GETAWAY

Gasper's Cove Mysteries Book 4

BARBARA EMODI

C&T PUBLISHING
Another Maker Inspired!

Publisher: Amy Barrett-Daffin

Creative Director: Gailen Runge

Senior Editor: Roxane Cerda

Cover Designer: Mariah Sinclair

Book Designer: April Mostek

Production Coordinator: Zinnia Heinzmann

Illustrator: Emilija Mihajlov

Published by C&T Publishing, Inc., P.O. Box 1456, Lafayette, CA 94549

Library of Congress Control Number: 2024942936

Printed in the USA

10 9 8 7 6 5 4 3 2 1

Gasper's Cove Mysteries Series

• *Book 1* •
Crafting for Murder

• *Book 2* •
Crafting Deception

• *Book 3* •
Crafting with Slander

• *Book 4* •
Crafting a Getaway

DEDICATION

To Steve Morgan for sharing his kindness and enthusiasm for gaming with miniatures with me.

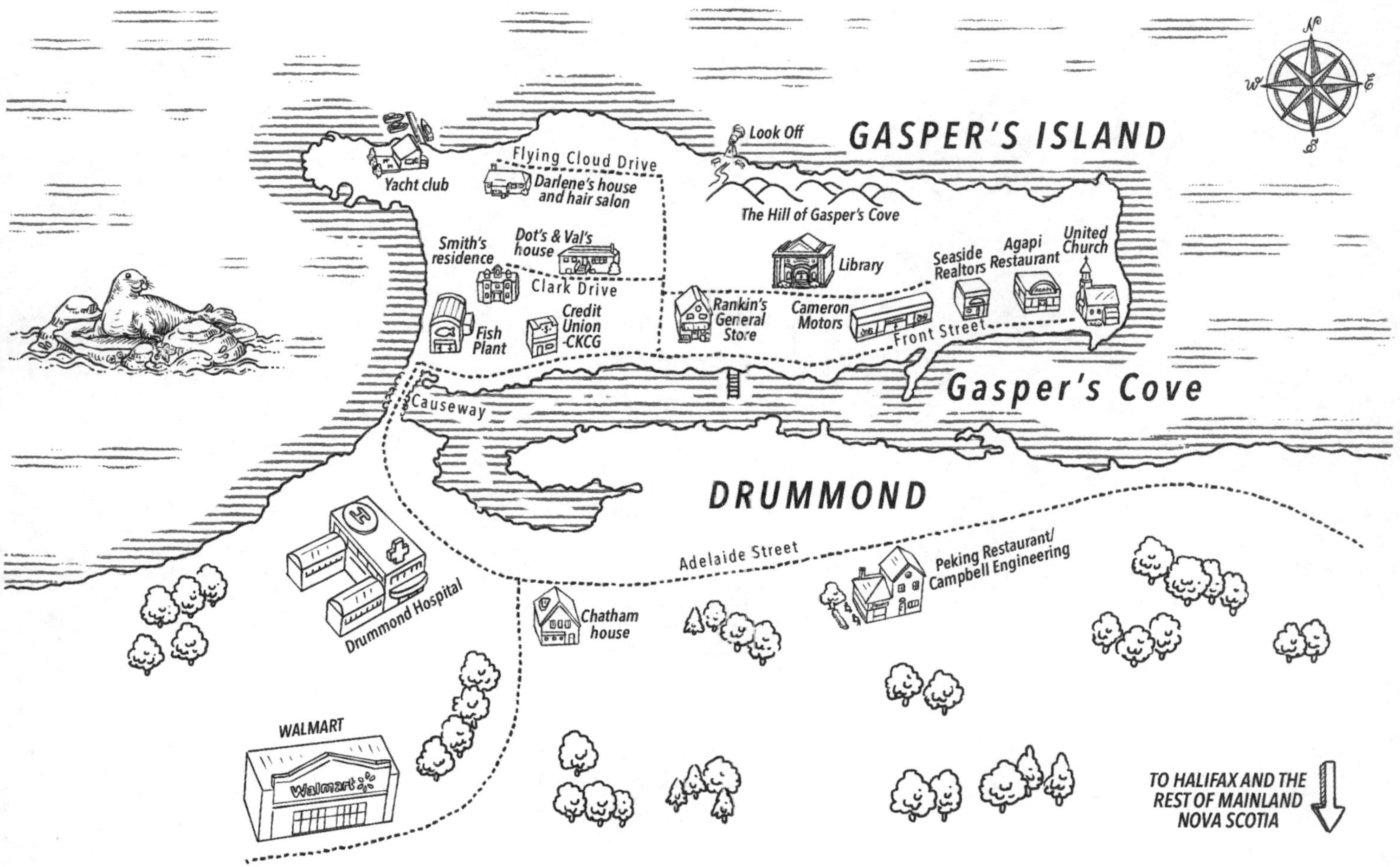
GASPER'S ISLAND
Look Off
Flying Cloud Drive
Yacht club
Darlene's house and hair salon
The Hill of Gasper's Cove
Smith's residence
Dot's & Val's house
Clark Drive
Library
Seaside Realtors
Agapi Restaurant
United Church
Fish Plant
Credit Union -CKCG
Rankin's General Store
Cameron Motors
Front Street
Causeway
Gasper's Cove
DRUMMOND
Adelaide Street
Peking Restaurant/ Campbell Engineering
Drummond Hospital
Chatham house
WALMART
TO HALIFAX AND THE REST OF MAINLAND NOVA SCOTIA

CHAPTER ONE

The woman leaned forward over the counter and handed me a gray baby cardigan.

"For my neighbor's daughter." She looked past me to the big semicircular window and its view of the sea. "This place is the best-kept secret in the country," she pronounced. "Here, in the middle of nowhere. Do you know how lucky you are?"

"I think we do," I said. I took the small sweater and folded tissue paper over the tiny garter-stitched cuffs, pearl buttons, and miniature buttonholes. "You mean the store? It's been in the family for generations. We always sold tools and fishing gear. The crafts are new." I slid the little package into the brown bag I had stenciled with *Crafters' Co-op, Gasper's Cove, Nova Scotia.* We made these gray baby clothes because they sold, but our older knitters couldn't figure it out. What is wrong with yellow, turquoise, or even melon, they asked? Something more cheerful, like the babies themselves.

My customer passed me a hundred-dollar bill. On her left hand was an engagement ring with a stone so substantial, it was set deep into the gold, with no need for a pronged setting to amplify its size. On her right hand were even more shimmering stones. But I saw no family ring like the ones local women wore, with a birthstone for each member of the immediate clan. "Your store's a hidden treasure. So quaint. So simple," the woman said, "but so is everything else. The coast, this island—I didn't know places like this existed." She ran her fingers over the smooth contours of a hand-carved driftwood bird. "You know, I used to make things myself. Years ago." She sounded wistful. "I want to get back into it. Release my creative energy. Maybe the retreat will help."

The retreat? This got my attention. I'd organized the crafters for the first one next month. Was this lady one of our students? I was thrilled. I'd ask her name and look her up on the list.

"I think you are going to enjoy yourself," I said, more loudly than intended. "August is a lovely time of year. We've got great workshops. Quilting, knitting, rope weaving ..."

Shadow, the store cat, interrupted me. She jumped up onto the counter and reached across to bat a cross-stitched bookmark onto the floor. Leaning over the edge, she studied it, pivoting her beautiful ears backward so she wouldn't miss any of this conversation. She lifted a paw to stroke her whiskers and to cover her smirk.

"August?" The woman was puzzled, irritated. "You've got that wrong. It's next week. My fiancé's here for meetings. I decided to show up, surprise him, and do something for myself." The clasp on an ostrich leather handbag snapped open. "Here, let me show you," she said, smoothing out a computer printout with her fancy hands so I could read it:

Escape to beautiful Gasper's Cove!

Learn new creative skills from local experts at a Crafter's Retreat

Starting Monday, July 8th

Sign up for one or all of the following workshops at the historic Bluenose Inn.

Monday: North Atlantic knitting. Thrummed mittens with Bob Willett.

Tuesday: Gifts from the sea. Woven reclaimed lobster rope wreaths with Sylvie Kulberg.

Wednesday: Quilting at the Cove. A table runner with Catherine Walker.

For further information, please contact Valerie Rankin.

"It sounds great doesn't it?" My visitor's face gleamed with retinol, excitement, and hope.

"Terrific," I said, forcing a smile. I needed time to think. Shadow jumped down to stickhandle the bookmark across the store's hundred-year-old floorboards. "You wouldn't want to miss something like that," I muttered. I felt seasick. This woman was here a month early. How had that happened?

My customer, now my student, was oblivious to my panic.

"Hey," the woman said, snapping her glittering fingers. "I have an idea. You're crafty." She waved a black-linen arm around the Co-op. "Why don't you come too? Learn something new? Maybe they have space. Call this Valerie Rankin person and find out. Do you know her?"

I nodded.

Yes, I did.
She was me.

The customer's name was Laura Sanders. By the time she left, I knew that her fiancé was Parker Wallace, very wealthy, very important, and head of East-West Media. Laura, clearly impressed with herself for snagging such a great catch, told me Parker was in Nova Scotia to explain to small rural newspapers that his take-over was the best thing that ever happened to them, despite what anyone else might say.

I also learned from Miss Sanders that her fiancé's meetings were to be held at an inn I knew as well as I knew I was not hosting a craft retreat there next week. The Bluenose Inn was owned by my cousin Rollie Rankin and Catherine Walker, the town's former librarian. Catherine had gone into business with Rollie to keep herself busy while she waited for him to propose.

The ramifications of the scheduling disaster crashed over me. Who else thought the retreat was next week, not in August? What if other students showed up at the Inn for workshops that didn't exist? Who would trust someone to run classes if they couldn't keep the dates straight?

There was only one thing to do. This was an emergency.

As soon as Laura Sanders left, I called Darlene.

Darlene was a cousin on my mother's side and my best friend. If I was in trouble, she would know how to get me out of it. She always did. Every time.

Darlene picked up on the first ring. She listened calmly while I told her what had happened.

"How do I fix this?" I asked her. "I had such big plans. It's a mess."

"Give me a second while I think," Darlene said. This wouldn't take long. My cousin was good on her feet. She had lots of practice from decades spent standing behind the chair in her basement beauty salon and then from door-to-door campaigning to be deputy mayor.

"First, how did you miss this?" she asked. "Weren't you keeping track of registrations?"

"I was. Sort of," I pulled the book with the names of those who had signed up out of a drawer. "I have it all here. The receipts from everyone who came in to pay. I'm looking at it now. All the dates are for the first week in August. Exactly when I told Catherine we'd be there."

"That sounds okay," Darlene said. "But what about this woman? You said she had something printed off the computer?"

"Yes, she did." Then, it hit me. "The town. I sent them the information for the website. You know, 'Things to See and Do in Gasper's Cove'? Did I get that wrong?" I pulled the Co-op's old laptop toward me and clicked on the page.

"Oh, shoot!" I said. "That's the problem. I must have made a mistake when I filled in the form. Switched the months and dates, put them in backward. It's dealing with tourists. I got used to the American way: month, date, and year. Not like we do it in Canada: date, month, and year. I changed August 7 to July 8. What an idiot." I had ignored numbers my whole life. This was their revenge.

I signed in and clicked the registration button. It was worse than I thought. "I don't believe this. There are four women signed up for next week. What am I going to do? The

Inn's booked for some corporate media thing. Catherine's my quilting instructor, and she's going to be busy. Next week can't happen. I don't have teachers. I don't have space. But I can't cancel on these ladies. That will kill my reputation before I even have one."

"Relax. So, you made a mistake. Big deal," Darlene said. "This might be better than you think."

"How's that?" I asked. My cousin had been an optimist, almost to the point of being ridiculous, ever since we had met, just outside our mothers' wombs. But if there was a bright side to this, I couldn't see it.

"It's obvious." I could tell Darlene was proud of herself. "You find a way to make it work. Don't worry about space, I'll find you something in the municipality. You just make sure this first group gives you rave reviews. That way, you can advertise the next session as 'back by popular demand.' So popular you had to run two sessions."

No wonder Darlene had made it in politics. I knew I had been spun, but it gave me a sliver of hope. The waves of anxiety were now ripples. "You can find me a nice place?" I asked.

"A great place," Darlene said. "I'll pull strings. Now, remind me. Teachers? Who are they? You'll need to get them organized too."

"Okay. Sylvie's making wreaths out of reclaimed lobster rope."

There was silence on the other end of the line except for the sound of meowing in the background. Darlene had a large and floating population of rescue cats. I had lost count of how many.

"Reclaimed rope?" she asked. "You mean from boats? Where does Sylvie get that?"

"From some guy with a blimp who's mapping algae. He says it's washed up all along the coast. He sees it from the air and picks it up." I knew this sounded crazy. "He's part of Sylvie's eco network," I explained. "They met at the Great Beach Clean-Up. Her rope wreaths sell, better than the ones she made out of plastic debris. Don't knock it."

"I won't." Darlene kept moving. "Who else you got?"

"Catherine is doing a table runner. It's cute, waves and little whales." Who could teach that workshop now? "And Bob Willett is doing the knitting class. Mitts, you know, the ones with the wool roving inside."

"Right. Nothing warmer." Darlene paused. "I didn't know Big Bob knit." I heard tiny pellets dropping into tin bowls. The meowing stopped.

"He does, very well. He dyes his wool with something called rescued lichen. He came up with the idea himself," I added.

"Sounds like something he'd do," Darlene said. In a community full of eccentrics, Big Bob was respected as the master of them all. "Alright, this is the plan. I find you a space, you round up the teachers. Then, let those four ladies know there has been a change of venue. If I were you, I would run out and have a word with Rollie and Catherine. Someone might show up on Monday by mistake. They need to know the town advertised something that isn't happening at the Inn. But get things organized first. Catherine is someone you go to with a solution, not a problem."

"She's not going to understand this," I said. "Catherine doesn't like the unexpected. She likes the alphabetical. She'll kill me when I tell her what happened."

"I doubt it," Darlene said. "No one gets killed over an innocent mistake."

CHAPTER TWO

After I hung up from my call with Darlene, I went down to the main floor of the store to collect Toby, my golden retriever. Toby came to work with me most days and spent his time as a greeter on the old recliner near the front door. We usually walked down to the store on the waterfront from our house up on the hill, but if I were going to see Catherine, I would need the car. So, I clipped the leash to Toby's collar, and we headed back up home.

As soon as we turned the corner to our street, I could see the handle of a cloth bag hanging out under the lid of my mailbox ahead.

Catherine had already been there.

The bag, I knew, would contain a book, most likely nonfiction, because that was what Catherine liked best, dropped off for me to read and for us to discuss. Last week, she had left *Big Magic* by Elizabeth Gilbert. That book made the interesting argument that ideas were living things cruising around the universe on the lookout for someone to take them in. That made sense but had taken time to digest.

I was relieved to see that today she'd left me something more practical, a cookbook, *Wartime Recipes from the Maritimes 1939–1945*.[1] I wanted to sit down and start reading, but I knew I had a crisis to manage first. So, I opened the front door, ushered Toby in, put the book on the table in the entry, picked up my keys, and headed out.

I decided to call Catherine as I drove to tell her I was coming. Stuart Campbell, my technical consultant, since I didn't know what else to call him, had rigged up my phone so it connected to the speaker in my car. I snapped on my seatbelt, tapped a button, and called the Inn. As I waited for someone to pick up, I thought about Stuart, the single father of one of our junior crafters. I knew him as the consulting engineer who had helped me renovate the second floor of the store. Stuart knew me as a woman with a nice dog and not much practical sense. The only person who thought there was more than this to say about us was Darlene.

The phone at the Inn went to voicemail. I left a message. Was there anyone else I should call?

My other instructors. Could they teach next week on such short notice?

I had to find out. My next call was to Sylvie, my wreath-weaving teacher, who, like many of the Gasper's Cove crafters, lived across the causeway in Drummond.

"Hey, Val, how's things?" Sylvie sounded distracted. The sound of running water blurred her words.

"Fine, but I need your help. What are you doing right now?" I asked, raising my voice. "I'm on the way to the Inn, but mind if I swing by your place first?"

---

1. Devonna Edwards, Wartime Recipes from the Maritimes 1939–1945 (Halifax, Nova Scotia: Nimbus Publishing, 2001).

"Sure, no problem," Sylvie answered. "The kids are at camp. The dogs are out digging up the backyard. I'm here by myself. What's going on?"

"More than I can explain over the phone," I said. As I crossed the causeway, I watched a slight breeze whisk the water into peaks. Yes, black-linen Laura was right. This was a special place to live.

I refocused. "How much rope do you have?"

"Lots. I'm washing the salt and seaweed out of a bunch of it so it will be soft enough to work." Sylvie sounded curious. "Why do you need rope?'

"I'll tell you when I get there."

"Okay. I still have coffee in the pot. See you soon."

It didn't take long for me to get to Sylvie's house. Drummond was bigger than Gasper's Cove, with a population of 5,000 to our 2,000, but the communities were only minutes apart, separated by a narrow band of water. As the bigger town, Drummond even had a subdivision, something we did not, built in the 1960s when the fish plant was still active. Sylvie's house was in the middle of that development in a style popular then. It was a small home on a big lot, a low bungalow with a roof that slanted down on one side to make a carport that sheltered the side door everyone used as the main entry. The last time I'd been at her house, there had been mason jar–lid wind chimes dangling from the eaves. Today, the drain spout was covered in a giant knitted sock.

I parked on the street. Sylvie's van and a truck that belonged to her basement tenant, RCMP officer Dawn Nolan, were in the driveway. I passed both vehicles as I walked through the carport and up to the side door.

Sylvie was waiting for me at the entry, in a small landing between the three steps to her kitchen and the flight of stairs down to the basement.

"Come on in," she said, pushing open the screen door and leading me to the kitchen. Plastic laundry baskets full of coils of thick, wet, nylon rope were queued in a line from the hallway across the linoleum floor to the sink. "What's this about?" she asked.

Sylvie had painted each of her kitchen chairs a different color. I chose a pink one and sat down. A large calico cat lying in the middle of the table opened one eye, regarded me, then closed it, and went back to sleep.

"That's a lot of rope you got there," I noted. "I heard you get it from that guy who flies the remote-control blimp. Is that true?"

"Yes, it is. Larry Beal. He works for some kind of algae-mapping foundation," Sylvie explained. "Kind of an environmental watchdog. He sends the blimp up and follows it along on land. He sees everything. That's why he started picking up the rope."

"I guess that's useful," I said.

"It is if you're interested in algae, which a lot of people aren't. That's probably why Larry doesn't have many friends. It's all he can talk about." Sylvie pushed aside a dripping laundry basket with her foot. She pulled out a purple chair and sat down. "Now, what's going on?"

I took a big breath. "There's been a mistake with the dates for the retreat. I've got an extra group coming next week by mistake. I'm trying to see if I can take care of them. The Inn's busy, but Darlene is finding me a place, and I need teachers." I tried to suppress the pleading tone in my voice. "Any chance you can do your workshop on Tuesday?"

"Tuesday?" Sylvie asked. "I've got something on. Golf lessons. A birthday present from my husband. He says all the other navy wives play. He has this idea I'll fit right in." She rolled her eyes.

My heart sank. I didn't know one other person alive who knew how to make rope wreaths. "Don't worry," I said. "Just thought I'd ask."

Sylvie looked confused. "Didn't you hear me? Golf. I'd *love* an excuse not to do it. I'll tell him this is an emergency." Her face brightened with a new thought. "If I can put these lessons off long enough, the golf season will be over. I'm not going to let you down, Val. Count me in. Tuesday it is."

"Are you sure?"

"Couldn't be more sure. It would be nothing to get ready." Sylvie pointed to the wet rope in the baskets, unbothered by the puddles on her kitchen floor. "I'll bring in the dogs and put this load out on the grass in the sun. It will be dry by tomorrow. Tuesday's not a problem."

I wanted to hug her. "I owe you for this one," I said. We both knew that was true. I glanced through the archway to the living room and its big picture window. My knitting teacher, Bob Willett, lived right across the street with his brother and sister-in-law.

"Maybe I should go over to see Bob while I'm here," I said. "Find out if there's a chance he can do Monday."

"No need to go anywhere," Sylvie said. "He's downstairs. Bob comes over to play toy soldiers and boats with Dawn." She saw the look on my face. "No, that's not a euphemism.

That's exactly what they do." She looked down at her baskets of wet rope. "We all have our interests."

No one understood that better than me.

"Do you think I could go down and see him?" I asked.

"Sure. Why not?" Sylvie walked across the kitchen and using her best mother-of-three-children voice, bellowed down through the doorway, "Dawn, you've got company."

She turned to me. "Go right down. The only thing you're going to disturb is the Battle of the Atlantic."

I was glad Sylvie had prepared me for the scene in her basement. As soon as I was at the bottom of the stairs, I saw the couch and lone chair had been pushed hard up to the perimeter of the living area to make way for a very large, low coffee table. On that table was a map. Even from a distance, I recognized it. It was a detailed coastal survey map, the kind that Fisheries and Oceans Canada issued, of the Gulf of St. Lawrence and the Atlantic provinces—New Brunswick, Prince Edward Island, Newfoundland, and Nova Scotia. As I got closer, I could see that sweeping arcs had been drawn over the pale blue water in red pencil, down the St. Lawrence, around the large island of Newfoundland, and crisscrossed to aim at Nova Scotia and Halifax Harbor. Next to these lines were rows of tiny boats, some the light gray of naval vessels, others long black cylinders, with single, finned towers. On the worn faux leather couch in front of this strange arrangement was my mitt-knitting teacher, Big Bob Willett, and Officer Dawn Nolan, of the Royal Canadian Mounted Police. When they looked up and saw me, they moved apart. I was interrupting something, a naval or romantic strategy, I wasn't sure which.

"Sorry to bother you." I walked over for a closer look at the map. "I can see you are busy. Sylvie thought it would be okay if I came down and talked to Bob. I need a favor."

"Not a problem," Dawn said. "Time we took a break. Can I get you something? Water? A tea?"

There were two pottery mugs close together on the edge of the table, carefully positioned on a pair of vintage coasters printed with Mounties on horseback. I pulled my eyes away and back to Bob.

"No, I'm fine, thank you. Look, there's been a mix-up. Some students are coming early for the workshops." I waited for Bob to ask why, and when he didn't, I gratefully continued. "Any chance you can pull together a session of your mitt class for this Monday?"

Bob repositioned one of the black miniatures before he spoke. I realized that the little boat was a replica of a submarine.

"I could probably help you out," Bob said, finally. "I have a few things to do, but nothing on that can't wait." He paused, and then he smiled. "Hey, I've just finished dyeing a batch of yarn. I used lichen I found under the trees. I wouldn't mind getting a group to knit it up and see how it looks."

"You should see his latest, it's really beautiful," Dawn interrupted. She started to pat Bob's knee, then withdrew her hand. "Woodsy colors, variegated."

"That's right." Bob blushed, pleased with the appreciation. "I was surprised at how nice it turned out. I used domestic ammonia this time instead of urine, which would be more traditional, to release the pigment. It worked nearly as good."

"Really?" I couldn't believe my luck, both that Bob could teach and that he had dyed the potential students' yarn nontraditionally. "That's amazing. I'll confirm the location. Start at ten?"

"You're on," Bob waited. He and Dawn Nolan were eager to get back to their tiny boats.

I looked down at the coffee table. "The Battle of the Atlantic?" I asked, quoting Sylvie, to be social.

Dawn Nolan leaned back. I saw she was wearing moss-colored hand-knitted socks. She placed a tiny gray navy ship on the map.

"No," she said, "closer to home. The Battle of the St. Lawrence, at the beginning of the war. The U-boats stalked anything on the surface, navy or merchant marine. We lost twenty-three ships, right under our noses. The objective was to tie up Canadian resources so they couldn't be sent to help out in Europe."

"Powerful psychological warfare," Bob added. "Everybody along the coast was sure they saw something. And every reported sighting had to be checked out, which diverted personnel. But what could they do? The longer the war went on, the more the idea that there was something evil out there under the water, waiting to get them, wore away at people's minds."

"Fear makes things real, even if they aren't there," Dawn said quietly. "I see that on the job all the time. You know, even Churchill said the only thing that scared him were the U-boats."

I looked at the map again. "Those red lines," I said, pointing to the map. "They're not tides, or fishing areas, or shipping lines, are they? That's where the submarines were hiding, wasn't it?"

"You got it," Bob said.

This was interesting, but I wondered why anyone, so many years later, would be down in a suburban basement plotting it all out. "So, you're reenacting the battle?" I asked. "Out of historical interest?" We all had hobbies. I sure had mine.

"There is more to it than that," Dawn said. "The *Kriegsmarine*, the German navy, didn't just sink ships. They also planted mines, right up to the mouth of the Halifax harbor, if you can believe it. They dropped off spies, and they were sent to pick up escaped POWs. I guess I am trying to understand what it felt like to be them, both the hunter and the hunted." She paused and placed another narrow black sub on one of the red lines. It was targeted directly to where we were now. She hesitated. "For me, it's personal, too."

I stared at her. What did she mean? The war had ended decades ago.

"Personal?" I asked.

"Yes. It was a kind of a family secret. No one wanted to talk about it. But I couldn't let it go. That's how I am." There was resignation in her voice. She looked over at Bob.

"Tell her," he said.

"My grandfather was on U-132." She looked at a small, thin sub pointed at our shore. "He spent the war not far from here, out of sight, just below the surface."

CHAPTER THREE

I stared at Dawn.

"Pastor Jäger?" I remembered Dawn's grandfather—we all did. He had been the local Lutheran minister. He had founded a summer camp for kids and had been the chief fundraiser for our assisted living residence, Seaview Manor.

"Yes. At the end of his life, my grandfather started to talk," Dawn explained. "He told quite the story." Bob moved closer to her. "This is how it started. His dad, my great-grandfather, was an engineer. Mercedes-Benz. Motorcycle division."

I knew nothing about anything with wheels. "Really? I thought they just made cars."

"Nope. My great-grandfather was head of the motorcycle design department." Dawn eyed me to make sure I was ready for what was coming next. "One weekend, he brought home a prototype, some new high-powered bike. At the time, my grandfather was sixteen. You can imagine how exciting that was." I thought of my own two boys as teenagers. I understood. "At any rate," Dawn continued, "one night, when the rest of the family was asleep, my grandfather snuck out and took the new motorcycle for a spin."

I had a premonition that this story wasn't going to end well. "So, what happened?" I asked.

Bob took over. "He crashed it. Hit a cattle crossing in the road and smashed the whole thing on a post. Dawn's grandfather was thrown clear, but the bike was totaled."

"You're kidding. What did he do?'

"Fathers were different then," Dawn sighed. "My grandfather said he knew there was no point going home because his dad would never forgive him." As she looked at me, I saw a shadow of resolution and sadness drift across her face. I wondered if her grandfather had looked like this when he told her this story. "So, he didn't go home. Not ever again. He kept walking until he came to Stuttgart. He went right into a recruiting office, lied about his age, and joined the navy. Then, the war started."

"And that's how he ended up in a U-boat?" I asked.

"Afraid so. One of the ones that patrolled these waters." Dawn smiled grimly. "And I guess one day they were so close that when he looked through the periscope, he could see the Nova Scotia coast. He told me that as soon as he saw it, he thought, if the Lord gets me out of here alive, I'm coming right back. Start over. And that's exactly what he did."

After I left Drummond and Sylvie's house, I crossed over to Gasper's Island and turned onto the north road that led to the Inn. As I drove, I looked across the road to the ocean. I tried to imagine how it felt to have lived here when the U-boat wolf packs were lurking under the water, watching.

It had never occurred to me that the men on those boats were afraid, too, or that they wanted to escape. I mulled over Dawn's story. Her grandfather had done a lot for the community. Yes, he had a past, but most of us did. Some of it we shared, and some of it we kept to ourselves.

My phone rang.

Darlene.

"I got you a space," she said. "The multipurpose room at the visitor's center is free. I went ahead and booked it."

I knew the room. It was perfect. It was inside the front doors of the Heritage Interpretive Centre building, next to where the last of the ferries that had connected Gasper's Island to Drummond on the mainland was docked. The building had light, a beautiful view of the water, and free parking.

"That's fantastic," I said. There was a rumble on the road behind me. "Was it hard to get?"

"Let's say that being deputy mayor helped. Gail Purves, who runs the center, wasn't a lot of help until I told her you needed something because of a problem at the Inn. That cheered her right up, and suddenly you had a room."

A large van with *Algae Coastal Mapping Project* on its side pushed past me. Larry Beal, Sylvie's rope supplier, was at the wheel. I didn't think he saw me.

"Cheered her up? What's that about?" I asked.

"Don't you remember her from the meeting?" Darlene asked. "The one where Rollie and Catherine lobbied to have the occupancy tax extended to private renters?"

"Sort of," I said. I vaguely remembered a debate about making things fairer for bed-and-breakfasts undercut by short-term rentals, but I'd been bored. I had knitted.

"She has a cottage she lets out to tourists," Darlene explained. "Rollie and Catherine made a good case. We expanded the tax. It's cost her money."

I heard a honk. A food truck, "Catch of the Day," passed me. I looked in the rearview mirror. Two more converted milk trucks, refitted to feed the hungry out of little windows, were closing in. One of them, "Schnitzel Express," blew its horn. The other, "It's All Greek to Me," did not, possibly because it was driven by a friend, George Kosoulas from the Agapi Restaurant. My low-gas light flashed. I looked at the dashboard. I was driving twenty miles below the speed limit, maybe in an uneducated attempt to stretch out my thinning gas supply, maybe to delay my arrival at an organizational disaster. I realized that Darlene was still talking.

"What did you say?" I asked. "Schnitzel Express" passed me in a swoosh of gravel. George was close enough behind me to wave. I waved back. "Sorry, there's a lot of traffic out here this morning. George is right behind me."

"I was just saying that Gail still hasn't forgiven Rollie and Catherine," Darlene paused. "Is he alone?"

Did she mean George?

"Looks like it," I told her. What did that have to do with anything? "Listen, I'm going to have to let you go. I'm at Rollie's now."

I hung up and made the turn into the Bluenose Inn's drive. I was surprised to see that the convoy of food trucks had turned, too, veering off onto the service road that led around to the back of the Inn. I continued straight ahead up to the main entrance.

It took a minute for me to find a place to park. The usually empty area off to the side of the horseshoe driveway that arched up to the old sea captain's mansion was full. In addition, two cars were parked on Rollie's lawn. One, a black Lexus SUV with Ontario plates, was on Catherine's flower bed.

I pulled in close to the edge of a ditch and got out of my car.

I looked at the front of the Inn and hesitated. I didn't feel up to talking to strangers. So, instead of climbing the steps to the glassed-in porch of the front entry, I made my way along the hedges to the back entrance. There, I was surprised to see a large figure jammed behind two propane tanks under the kitchen window.

"Rollie? What are you doing in there?" I asked.

"What does it look like?" my cousin answered. "I'm hiding. Taking a breather."

"From what?"

Rollie squeezed his large body out from between the two gas cylinders and looked up warily at the steps back into the Inn. "You mean from who. Rebecca Coates. The PR advance person they sent down for this conference thing to make sure everything is up to scratch. Which, apparently, it isn't." Rollie looked up with envy at the seagulls surfing the breeze off the ocean. "She timed us setting up the meeting room with a stopwatch. Like we were at some track-and-field event. She's calling the local news outlets 'profit centers.' She doesn't like our food. She doesn't like our carpet. She doesn't have enough bars on her phone. And then there was the mouse."

"The mouse?"

"The one running around her room. She tried to kill it with her clipboard, but it got away. I told her that's why we have a cat. She wasn't impressed."

I looked at the century-old wood siding of the old building. What did this Rebecca Coates expect? Out here, when the mice sidled in, the cats chased them out. It was an ancient system, and it was effective. I could see this was not a good time for me to tell Rollie about my doubling-up retreat issue or to ask his business partner to teach an extra table-runner class.

Above us, the screen door of the back porch snapped open.

"There you are," Catherine called out, looking down at us, hot and tense in the quilted vest that was her bed-and-breakfast host uniform. "Rollie, Miss Coates says our coffee is too weak. However, she travels with her own espresso machine. She's in the kitchen now." Usually as organized as the Dewey decimal system, Catherine looked like she had been hit by a bus. Or maybe a Lexus with Ontario plates. "Three other things. She wants us to get rid of all the flowers. She says the meetings have to be scent-free. And the extension cords have gone missing. Where did they go?" Catherine stopped and took four deep breaths to calm herself, in this case, ineffectively. "And why are the trucks here?" She waved a hand at the end of the property near the cliff. "One of the men said he was told we were having a food truck rally! As if. I asked George Kosoulas, and he said Rebecca called him at the restaurant. She told George she had a bunch of news people here for an all-dayer and was concerned about food. She was trying to organize other options. What's she talking about? We can handle anything."

Rollie and I climbed the stairs to the porch. My cousin reached over and straightened the name tag on Catherine's vest.

"Not to worry, my love," he said. "I'll talk to her. I'll empty the vases and see what's going on with these food people. You just relax. We'll get through this." I noticed my cousin was using his counselor's voice. In another life, Rollie had been a practicing psychologist. That training was handy now.

"If you say so." Catherine watched my cousin as he headed back into the building, a faint smile on her face. She looked at me. "I know why you're here," she said, her smile fading. "Darlene called to prepare me. You need a quilting teacher for next week. Obviously, I can't do it."

"I can see that," I said. "Do you know anyone else who could?"

Catherine looked surprised. "You. It's an easy project. I have the kits all made up and copies of the instructions in the office. You'll be fine. Anyone can quilt."

I opened my mouth to say maybe anyone except me. I was better with two sleeves than with a hundred little pieces, but before I could get the words out, Rollie was back. His face was pale under his beard, his blue eyes wide under his bushy eyebrows.

"Call 911," he said.

Catherine snapped into action, pulled out her phone, and dialed. "Why, what's happened?" she asked.

"I'll show you. Just tell them to get here as soon as they can," Rollie said, "then come in. Be quiet. The kitchen." Rollie and I went into the building. We left Catherine on the back step, talking into her phone. As I walked down the hall, I noticed an odd smell in the air.

"Here," Rollie said. I followed my cousin into the room to the left of the back entrance. He reached behind me and shut the door.

I saw why.

I'd never met Rebecca Coates, public relations professional for East-West Media, in person. Now, I never would.

But that didn't mean I couldn't see her, like I did now. I certainly saw her in her leather four-inch heels, a pencil skirt, and a matching navy suit I knew had to be at least ten percent Lycra to fit that snugly.

Yes, there she was. On the kitchen floor of the Bluenose Inn, with a two-tiered stove-top espresso coffeemaker in one French-manicured hand. There she was, in front of the dishwasher, the new one installed under the counter, right below the window with a lovely view of the sea.

A view she couldn't see. There she was, the PR lady from Ontario, down on the green floor, flat on her back, in a shallow pool of water, her hair splayed out around her, her blue eyes wide under impossibly long lashes, staring up at the high ceiling of the old Inn's most hard-working room. Lying there, very still, in the quiet way a body has when the person inside it has moved on.

No, Rebecca Coates and I would never meet. Because some time, just before I arrived, she had already left the kitchen.

CHAPTER FOUR

The kitchen door opened. Catherine walked into the room. George Kosoulas was right behind her.

"Tell me what's going on," Catherine said. "Why did I have to call 911?"

Rollie pointed to the motionless figure on the floor.

Catherine froze. She'd spent her life ordering the world into predictable patterns. She hadn't predicted this. She opened her mouth to speak and forgot to close it. Next to her, George stepped forward and then back. With effort, he composed himself.

"We have to do something," I said. I started to move to the pool of water under the late but very well-dressed Ms. Coates. George threw out an arm to stop me.

"Don't. I've seen this before. No one touch anything." George's voice was calm, but his eyes were intense. "Rollie, cut the power." The two men exchanged a look. Rollie nodded and hurried out.

"Why?" I asked. My voice sounded like it belonged to someone else.

"I think she's been electrocuted. We can't go near her until the power is off." George looked at Catherine. "You called, right?"

"I did," she said. "Emergency Health Services and the RCMP are on their way."

The door opened behind her. Rollie was back. "Done," he said.

As soon he heard this, George walked carefully over to where Rebecca Coates lay. Then, with a light, almost tender touch, he reached down and put two fingers to the side of her neck. He stood up. His look answered the question we all had. "We should go outside," he said.

When the four of us were in the hall, Rollie pulled out a ring of keys and locked the kitchen door.

We didn't have to wait long for help to arrive, although it seemed like we did. Rollie stayed at the reception desk in case guests came by. The rest of us went out through the glassed-in vestibule to stand on the front porch.

The first to arrive was the Emergency Health Services ambulance. Two paramedics rushed toward us. Catherine led them into the kitchen. One of them was Jason Willett, Big Bob's brother.

That left George and me to wait for the RCMP.

"I can't believe this," I said. "You said you saw something like this before. How? When? What do you think happened?"

"Hard to say." George looked out at the ocean beyond the large lawn as if it had some answers. "But as soon as I walked into that room, I had a flashback. One summer, when I went to work in a restaurant in Montreal, the owner had rigged up extension cords on the floor under the station with the mixers. One of the cleaners was washing the floor after we closed. There was water and a short in one of the cords. We found him the next morning. He looked like she did."

"That's terrible," I said. "You were young then, weren't you?" George, Darlene, and I had gone to high school together. Summer jobs in larger restaurants had been part of his dad's plan to get George ready to take over the Agapi some day.

"Nineteen," George said, running his hand through his black hair, now flecked with gray. He'd always been a good-looking boy growing up, with big dark eyes the mothers loved. He was one of those men who became more handsome with time, as the lines of experience added character to their faces. But right now, George looked older than his age.

We heard the sound of sirens on the main road. Moments later, an RCMP cruiser appeared. It parked in the driveway in front of the main entrance, and two officers climbed out. Both of them were young and new to me. Wade Corkum, the detachment's long-standing senior officer, was away. He had taken personal leave to help an old hockey buddy with rookie development with the Toronto Maple Leafs. Considering what he'd been through the year before, he'd earned the break. While he was away, Dawn Nolan was the senior officer in the detachment. I expected we'd see her here soon.

As he climbed the stairs to the porch, the younger of the officers seemed to read my mind. "We called the boss. She's on her way. I see the paramedics are here. Where do we go?"

"I'll show you," George said. "Come with me."

Left on my own, I sat down on the porch swing. I had no desire to go into that building again, not after what I'd seen in the kitchen. I realized I was shaking, and my knees felt weak. The door opened, and Catherine came out and sat beside me. She reached out a foot and slowly pushed the swing back and forth as if the rhythm soothed her and helped restore order in her mind.

"I don't believe it," she said, finally. "Our first season. And now one of our guests, our most demanding guest, is dead. Was this our fault?"

"Accidents happen," I offered. It was the best I could do. "They'll figure it out."

Catherine started twisting her watch with her fingers. Her eyes were unfocused as she scrambled to make sense of what she'd seen. "I should have gone into the kitchen with her, made her coffee. That's what a good innkeeper would do. But I didn't. I just wanted her out of the way while I tried to deal with the fiancée."

"The fiancée?" I asked.

"I shouldn't say anything, not now, but it was so awkward." It was clear Catherine was too upset to care what she said.

"Awkward?" I asked.

"They came down early, just the two of them, for the weekend. Mr. Wallace and Ms. Coates, to get ready for the meetings, at least that's what he said. I guess 'public relations' is what they are calling it these days." Catherine paused, then kept going. "This isn't a big place. I do the rooms. The ones that need making up." She looked at me to make sure I knew what she was saying.

I did.

"Laura Sanders? That's the fiancée?" The lady in black linen from the store with the gray baby cardigan? My next-week sewing student?

"Yes," Catherine answered, distracted. "She showed up at reception today. No reservation because her fiancé was already here. She said she wanted to surprise him."

"And was he surprised?"

"What do you think? She was the last person he and the girlfriend wanted to see."

I let this sink in. "And if there hadn't been an issue with the dates for the retreat, Laura wouldn't even be here. I feel sort of responsible for putting you in the middle of this."

Catherine looked at me sideways and waited.

"I'll make it up to you," I said. Catherine had enough on her mind. "I'll do that table-runner class. I'll learn how to quilt."

As soon as the door of her truck slammed open, I knew that Dawn Nolan with the toy boats was gone and that Officer Nolan of the RCMP had arrived on the job. With a quick impersonal nod to me, Nolan strode up to Catherine and asked to be shown the kitchen. I followed them into the Inn. Rollie was at the front desk.

"What's going on?" I asked.

"Not sure. We have a few folks in the conference room. They've put a man on the door to keep them there and sent another one out to talk to the food truckers."

I looked down the hallway and saw a Mountie standing stiffly on guard in front of a double door, his arms crossed over his chest. Through the open window, I heard the raised voices of cooks on wheels who were being told not to leave.

"What happens now?" I asked.

Rollie grimaced. "They're bringing the ambulance around the other side to take her out that way. They were just waiting for Officer Nolan to arrive and sign off on it."

"Nothing the paramedics could do?" I asked. We both knew there wasn't.

Rollie shook his head.

The door to the conference room flew open. A tall, balding man barreled out, slamming his white piqué golf shirt with its gold club crest into the young officer's flat black bullet-proof vest.

"Where's my PR gal? Why aren't we allowed out of this room?" the man demanded. "Who's in charge here? Let me speak to them!"

The kitchen door opened. Nolan came out and then slowly and deliberately walked down the hall.

"I got this," she said to her subordinate when she reached him. "Your PR *gal*?" Nolan asked the indignant man in the private club golf shirt. "You mean Ms. Coates?"

"That's the one," the man spat back. "Where is she? I need power for my presentation. There are no extension cords in that room. Not anywhere. We looked. I sent her to find them. And to get me a decent coffee."

Nolan looked at the newcomer without expression. "Your name, sir? And your relationship to Ms. Coates?"

"Wallace. Parker Wallace. East-West Media. I pay her salary. The extension cords are her job."

Nolan looked at Rollie. "Is there a room I can use?"

"Our office?" he suggested, motioning to the door marked "Manager" behind the counter.

Nolan nodded, then turned to the young officer.

"I'm going to speak to this gentleman. Don't let anybody else leave. We'll need statements." Outside, I heard the crunch of gravel. An emergency services ambulance was pulling in close to the building. Catherine walked over to the front window and turned the sign that hung there to *Closed.*

Rollie turned around, opened the door of the manager's office, and stepped aside. Officer Nolan motioned for Parker Wallace to go in.

"This better be good," Wallace fumed. Pushing past Rollie, he knocked a stack of "Canada's Ocean Playground" brochures onto the floor. He didn't look back, and he didn't pick them up.

CHAPTER FIVE

As soon as the door of the manager's office swung open again, I could see that Nolan was angry. It was in the tension of her shoulders and the tight line of her mouth. Death offended the RCMP officer, and she wasn't going to let anyone get away with it.

"Mr. Parker, that's all for now," she said to the man whose PR gal was never coming back. "We'll be in touch."

Wallace nodded, then faded off down the hall. His strut was gone. Nolan watched him go. She seemed satisfied, as if some question no one had asked had been answered.

She turned to me. "Can you tell me what brought you here today?"

"I came to talk to Catherine about a table runner," I said. My mission sounded so trivial. "For the workshops I'm trying to throw together."

"Right," Nolan said. "Like you asked Bob to do his mitts. When you arrived, it would have been just before Ms. Coates died. Is that correct?"

Why did that matter? "I guess it must have been," I answered. I thought of George. "It was an electrical shock, wasn't it? Only a terrible accident?" I asked. I wanted confirmation that the bad news was finished.

"An accident?" Nolan hesitated slightly. "Too early to say. We'll see what the evidence brings in."

Officer Nolan kept me around the reception desk until it was clear I had nothing useful to tell her. I was relieved when she said I could leave. I looked around and felt I didn't know where I was anymore. The Inn, once so familiar, suddenly looked off-kilter, crooked, as if the whole building had been tipped over at an angle by events that should never have happened. My legs wobbled as I walked toward the front door. The floor felt uneven under my feet, and for a moment I thought I was going to slide across the old boards and into a wall. The feeling scared me. I wanted out. I wanted flat grass. I wanted to look at a sky that looked like it had before. I wanted to be thinking about what I would make for dinner, about walking my dog. I wanted to be as far away as possible from the image of a woman who had died with an espresso pot in her hands.

I wanted to go home.

But as much as I wanted that, I knew I couldn't go back to my safe little bungalow yet. The business that had brought me to the Inn still had to be done. Numb, I retreated to the motions of normal life and my obligations. So, back in my car, instead of heading back up the hill to my house, I left Gasper's Cove and drove back across the causeway to talk to Gail Purves.

The Drummond-Gasper's Cove Historical Interpretive Centre Gail managed was on the waterfront on the Drummond side, beside the old ferry that had once connected our two communities. The building contained three spaces: an exhibition room, with its display of relics of old schooners in glass cabinets; a combined welcome area and gift shop; and a multipurpose room. This last was used to host bus tours, public meetings, and wedding receptions. If all went well, next week it would also accommodate makers of table runners, wooly-on-the-inside mitts, and wreaths woven from lobster rope. All that was left to do was to confirm the arrangements.

I arrived at the center as two carloads of tourists with Massachusetts plates were leaving. I waved to them, walked up the wooden ramp to the building, and pulled open a heavy glass door. Inside, the reception area was empty, but off to the side, I saw Gail bustling around the gift shop, refolding the stacks of made-in-China tea towels. She stopped when she saw me, crossed her arms, and waited for me to come to her.

"Valerie Rankin. Not surprised to see you here today," she said. "I guess you're here about the multipurpose room. Must be nice to have a relative who's deputy mayor."

"It is," I said, pretending the dig was well intended. "It was so good of you to make arrangements for my group at such short notice." I dug deep and pulled out a smile. The truth was the day had seriously depleted my reservoirs of charm.

Uncharmed, Gail glared at me, indifferent to the *Ciad Mille Failte* ("a hundred thousand welcomes") sign hanging behind her. "That room was supposed to be repainted this week," she said. "Who knows when I'll get that done now."

She paused, as if waiting for a rescheduling suggestion from me. When none came, she sighed and pulled a key from the pocket of her Nova Scotia tartan vest. "Since you're here, we might as well go have a look," she said.

As I followed her out of the gift shop and to the meeting room, I realized how little I knew about Gail. That felt odd. I was used to knowing everything about everybody, and if I didn't know a person well, I always knew someone who did. Except for Gail. She'd come from away—"New England" was as specific as she'd get—and if she had any friends, I hadn't met them. I had no idea why a middle-aged woman with a white bob and bright red lipstick would want to spend her days explaining a past that wasn't her own to anyone who dropped by. It didn't make sense. Some fact was missing.

And whatever that fact was, Gail wasn't going to share it with me. Instead, she pushed past me in her rubber-heeled wedge shoes and slammed open the door of the multipurpose room, adding a dent to the wall behind it. She offered me a key and seemed reluctant to let it go. "Make sure you leave things the way you found them," she instructed, like a mother leaving a child with a babysitter they didn't trust. "I mean that."

"Of course," I said, following her meekly into the room. "Just as I found it." I looked around. Just as I found it wouldn't be hard. Everything in the empty space, from the metal-legged tables to the stacks of plastic-seat chairs, seemed to have been designed for indestructibility.

Gail hesitated as she assembled her next line. "This better be all you need," she said. "Because it's all we've got."

"This is great," I reassured her. The room didn't matter—the view did. The spectacular sight of the water between here and Gasper's Cove would more than make up for this spartan interior. "This will be fine. The first two workshops are knitting and rope weaving. All we need for those are tables and chairs. Wednesday, the last day, I'll be teaching quilting." I stumbled over the words; too bad I had never quilted. "And all we'll need for that is power. For the sewing machines and irons." How hard could quilting be? I knew fabric.

"Irons?" Gail stared at me as if she'd never heard the word before. "I assume you'll bring your own. We don't have any of those here. Why would we? Nobody irons these days."

I let this pass. Everyone I knew ironed. Everyone. Anyone who sewed or quilted had to.

Gail had another thought. I could tell it annoyed her even more than the irons. "You're not thinking of bringing food, are you?" she asked, making room for "no" as the only answer. "I can't have the mess. We allow professional caterers only in this facility, and we use those for the big events." She smiled as she delivered her punch line. "But from what Darlene told me, this is not going to be a *big* event."

Food. How had I forgotten about that? No one could sew, craft, or quilt all day on an empty stomach.

"I can't have a group here, not even a small one, and not feed them," I blurted out. "Any suggestions?" I asked. I was desperate.

"I feel for you," Gail said, attempting and failing to look sympathetic. "I know why you're here. They let you down at the Inn, didn't they? Rollie Rankin and Catherine Walker promised and couldn't deliver. Big-time hospitality industry operators, trying to take out private renters, but they're not up to it, are they? That's why the big scramble. That's why Darlene came to me." Behind her glasses, a dark light glinted. Gail had a grandmother's figure, all bosom and thin legs. She looked like a mother hen, but had, I noticed for the first time, the canny eyes of a fox. "For food, the way I see it, you only have one option."

I waited. I knew I should defend Rollie and Catherine, but I let it go. I didn't have the energy. There was too much to say. This snippy woman had no idea what my cousin and Catherine were handling today, and I wasn't going to tell her. I wanted to go home.

"One option?" I asked. "What would that be?"

"Food trucks," Gail was pleased with herself. "We let some of them park here during the week near the water so they are close to the tourists. Take them to George and maybe the fish-and-chip guy. It will be lovely." She reached over and squeezed my forearm. I was surprised at how firm her grip was. "Do your workshops and then take your people out to the parking lot. Find them a nice place at the picnic table. Chase away the gulls and hope it doesn't rain." She let go of my arm. "It will be another first-class Rankin event. What could go wrong with one of those?"

I thought of Catherine's conference room and of Rollie's kitchen floor.

You'd be surprised, I wanted to say, but didn't. You'd be surprised.

CHAPTER SIX

Even though it wasn't, it felt like a long drive home. Being polite to Gail Purves had used up the last of me. Even on a good day, I hated change or confrontation, and this had not been a good day. I couldn't get the image of Rebecca Coates, victim of a tragic accident, out of my mind. And it seemed almost disrespectful to try. I knew there was nothing I could do, nothing I should have done, but that was no consolation. I wanted it all to be over. I needed to go blank. I needed to close my front door behind me, be alone with my dog, and eat chocolate ice cream.

But that would have to wait. When I turned into my street, I saw Stuart Campbell sitting on my front steps.

I'd met Stuart when I returned to the area after being away for twenty years in Halifax with a man no smart woman would have married. My experience with my former husband had made me wary of relationships with anyone who wasn't a child, an animal, or a relation. However, I had begun to wonder if it was time to make an exception for engineers from Drummond.

It wasn't as if I hadn't tried hard enough to find a flaw in Stuart. I had, but there was nothing there. He was one of those people who were exactly what they seemed to be, who couldn't pretend to be anything else if they tried, which he didn't. Stuart cared about what he cared about and not one bit about what he didn't. He wore an apron to cook, built his own boat, taught himself how to play the guitar, and tried to be two parents to a daughter who had only one. He always carried dog biscuits in his pockets, just in case. He strolled rather than walked. Stuart seemed to me to be a man who had everything he needed. So why, this close to suppertime, was he sitting on my front steps?

When I pulled into the driveway, he got up, walked over to the car, and opened the door.

"Are you okay?" he asked. "I heard what happened at the Inn. Tough stuff."

"You know?" I asked. "Already?"

"Yes, I do. Officer Nolan called me at home. She had some questions. The paramedics are pretty sure an electrical current was involved in this woman's death. They're going to investigate." Stuart glanced at my front window. Toby was on the couch, watching us, his leash and harness in his mouth. I noticed the muscles in Stuart's jaw contract. Something was wrong.

He nodded to the window and laughed tightly. "I came over to talk, but you better get that guy out. Mind if I walk with you?"

"Of course not. Glad for the company." I said, surprised this was true. I climbed the steps, opened the door, and let Toby out. The big retriever bounded out, did circles around Stuart, and then sat down so I could clip on his leash. "I wouldn't mind having someone to talk to myself. But you first. What's on your mind?"

Stuart waited until we had walked down to the elementary school on the corner to answer my question. Not making eye contact, he laid his hand on the monkey bars the kids climbed on and examined the structure with interest.

"You know I did the building inspection at the Inn before Rollie and Catherine bought the place, don't you?" he began. "They're friends of mine. If anything, I did more than my due diligence with that job. I didn't want them to get ripped off."

"I know. Rollie told me. But it was all fine, wasn't it?" I asked. "You wouldn't have let them buy the Inn if there had been problems, right?" I undid Toby's leash and let him run free onto the empty ball field.

"I wouldn't exactly say there weren't any problems." Stuart had switched to his professional voice, the same one he had used when we renovated the store. "Any old building is bound to have some issues. But I have to tell you, when those sea captains did a house, they built it like a ship. Solid as a rock. They used their own shipbuilders to do it. The craftsmanship is unbelievable. All Rollie had to do was put on a new roof, that's what I told him. But you know how it is." He picked up a ball some child, or dog, had left behind and threw it across the field for Toby.

"Not sure I do. What are you talking about?"

Stuart shrugged. "Time. A lot isn't up to code, not by today's standards. But the Inn was pretty good. The previous owners had put in new pipes, upgraded the plumbing, and replaced the wiring. Most of the big things that needed to be done had already been done." Toby trotted back to Stuart, ignoring me, and dropped the ball at his feet. Stuart picked it up and threw it again, farther than I could have thrown it. He looked at me and spoke slowly. "The wiring had been replaced," he repeated. "It was all new, I checked it. But when someone dies like that, the first thing everyone is going to wonder about is the wiring. And I signed off on it."

I focused on the sliver of silver on the horizon, out over the ocean, past the hills, and down at the wharf. "Are you second-guessing yourself now?" I asked, wishing I had a better way to say it.

"I am." Stuart's face was hard in the fading light of the late evening sun, a contrast with the curl of his dark hair. "I mean everything, my experience, my training, my whole life, to be honest, is about taking responsibility. I've gone over and over my reports. I'm sure I didn't miss anything. But now there's this other voice in my head. Was I careful enough? Was there something there I didn't see? Officer Nolan didn't ask me directly, but I knew that's what she was thinking."

"You mean, something in the wiring could have caused the accident?" I asked. The temperature had dropped, like it always did in the evenings near the ocean, even in the summer. I felt cold.

"Exactly." Toby dropped the ball at Stuart's feet and waited. Stuart picked it up and turned to me. I saw dread in his face. "What if I missed something?" he asked. "What if that woman is dead because I made a mistake?"

I wanted to help, but what did I have? "Let me think," I said. "I was there." I'd seen Rebecca Coates. What did I remember? I reeled back through all the images in my mind. I saw lobster-rope wreaths, ten-percent Lycra suits,

Catherine's quilted vest, an espresso pot, George's food truck, the water pooled on a linoleum floor, thrummed mitts, and then a manicured hand. Outstretched, reaching forward, the door of the dishwasher down. I felt a spark flare up, somewhere behind my eyes. A connection.

"The toaster," I said. "The curling iron. Like Darlene says."

"What?" Stuart was startled. "You aren't making any sense."

"Sorry. That's how my brain works." Stuart wouldn't know. I stored the world in pictures, in what Darlene called the junk drawer of my head. "The kitchen reminded me. Something Darlene says all the time. She read in *Canadian Living* that most house fires start because of shorts in appliances. That's why she unplugs everything every evening." It was true. I'd done the rounds with her when I'd spent the night. "Her house has never burned down," I added as evidence. "Maybe there wasn't any problem with the wiring. Maybe you didn't miss anything in your inspection. Maybe there was just a problem with a plug. An appliance."

Stuart looked at me as if he'd never seen me before. "Go on," he said. "Like what?"

I saw a blustering Parker Wallace storming out of the conference room looking for his PR gal. "I remember something," I said. "Just before the accident, her boss said he'd sent that poor woman out to find the missing extension cords. Later, George said he knew someone in a restaurant in Montreal who died because of an extension cord in some water." I was a genius. Stuart was in the clear. I'd figured it out. "That has to be it."

Stuart studied the clouds. The wind had picked up off the water and was pushing them inland. "I guess that's a possibility," he admitted. "Certainly, it's worth checking out. I'll give Officer Nolan a call and see if I can go out tomorrow. Have a look at that kitchen." He smiled his old smile, reached out, and laid a hand on my shoulder. "Thank you. This helps. Something concrete to follow up on. Something I can do. I need that."

Toby's tail slapped on the grass, and he nudged the ball toward us. Stuart picked it up and threw it.

High into the air. One last time.

CHAPTER SEVEN

I didn't sleep well that night. Walking home with Stuart had calmed me, but after he left, I could feel the tension inside build up again. I tried ice cream, I tried a bath, I tried a movie and worked on the socks I was knitting for my son in Toronto, but nothing helped. All night, I lay in the dark in my bed, unable to settle my thoughts. When I heard the birds start to sing in the morning, I surrendered and got up.

Toby and I trudged down to the kitchen. I let him out. As I watched my dog sniff his way around the yard, I noticed a pair of blue jays at the bird feeder hanging on the far end of the clothesline. A few years before, a jay had built a nest outside my kitchen window. At the end of the summer, the babies had flown away, like children, mine included, do. I'd put up the bird feeder in case those little birds ever wanted to come home. I wondered if the birds on the line were the same ones now.

I thought of my children. Kay, doing graduate work in Scotland. Paul, a pastry chef in New York. Chester, with the bank in Toronto. They'd been home again at the end of August. Lately, they'd talked about buying land and a cottage they could all use, a sort of summer family retreat. We'd see. Everyone had their own lives now. Anything could happen.

The coffee pot gurgled, and I poured myself a cup. Toby bounded around the yard in big loopy strides. His day was complete. I thought about mine. Today was Saturday. My workshops would start the day after tomorrow. Bob and Sylvie would do a good job the first two days. I was less sure about the class I'd be teaching. I had one weekend to learn to be a quilter, at least of the table-runner kind. I'd seen Catherine's sample, which was lovely. I knew her instructions would be perfect. I had made my own clothes for thirty years. I had taught garment sewing for at least half of that. How hard could quilting be? I was sure I had a quarter-inch foot somewhere.

But I needed to practice. I needed the kits. This meant another trip out to the Inn. If I hurried, I might run into Stuart. I called Toby in for his breakfast and went down the hall to get dressed.

As it turned out, by the time I arrived at the Bluenose Inn, Stuart had already come and gone.

"Sorry, you just missed him," Catherine said. "He and Officer Nolan were here for about an hour first thing. Stuart brought his tools, and they took pictures. The two of them were in the kitchen for quite a while and came out with a box full of something. I have no idea what. They won't let us in there yet. Good thing we have a coffeemaker and that little fridge in the breakfast room, or we'd be sunk. We still have guests."

My mind filled with questions. *What had Officer Nolan and Stuart taken out of the room? What if I was right? What if they'd found the missing extension cord? Or one of those short-circuited toasters Darlene worried about? What if I had come up with the answer? That would set Stuart's mind at ease, and I wanted that.* I straightened my spine. Now, if I could only learn to quilt before next Wednesday, I would be a star.

I noticed a tea tray laid out on the counter of the reception desk. I recognized the napkins. I'd made them myself as an inn-warming present.

"Taking that up to someone?" I asked Catherine.

"That's for me," a voice said. I looked up and saw Laura Sanders descend the elaborately carved staircase. "It's for Parker. He's too upset to come down."

Catherine lifted the tray to pass it to Laura. She'd folded my napkins into triangles and laid them next to the china cups, a little dish of local strawberries and blueberries, a teapot, and a plate of scones.

"Hope this helps," she said. "It must be awful for him. We're all in shock."

"We both are," Laura said. "We go back with Rebecca for years. I knew her first when she was a young reporter. She worked at my dad's TV station in Brandon, Manitoba. I used to read the news for him, then she took that over. I moved back behind the scenes, to do more of the technical production. It made sense. Rebecca was good in front of the camera, that's why she moved so easily into public relations. And it's why Parker kept her on when he took over the business. We agreed to wait to get married while he worked on expansion." Laura smoothed her black-linen tunic top. The gold charms on her bracelet jingled against the china teapot as she picked up the tray. "Such an efficient person. Rebecca did everything for Parker. Everything."

Catherine studied the scones uncomfortably.

It was time to talk about table runners.

"The quilt kits?" I asked Catherine. "I came to pick them up."

Laura Sander's head snapped up. Parker's tea was forgotten. "You mean for the class? The one I'm enrolled in? Can I take a peek?"

Catherine and I exchanged looks. I'd seen her table runner, it was beautiful, but I hadn't even read the instructions yet.

"Why don't I show you the sample?" Catherine asked Laura. "I have it in the office with the kits." She caught my eye. "I did the cutting for Valerie to help her out." Catherine went into the office and returned with a wicker basket full of resealable plastic bags. Catherine reached into the basket, lifted out a bright table runner, and spread it out on the reception desk.

"It's called *At the Cove*," Catherine explained. "I think it's a great class project. Quick to make, fused appliqués, all machine-stitched."

"I love it." Laura raised a pair of glasses from a chain on her chest to inspect the bright blue table runner with its cheerful border of white-capped waves, whales, and sailboats. She pulled out a kit and turned it over. "I see you've cut out the main fabric pieces and printed the appliqué shapes on the fusible web. Smart."

Some novice, I thought. For sure she had her own quarter-inch foot at home. Pretending to be efficient, I folded the table runner and laid it on the top of the basket. It seemed prudent to cut this conversation short before Laura asked me any questions.

"Thank you," I said, nodding to Catherine, to indicate she deserved some credit rather than, as we both knew, all of it. "It's going to be fun. Come to the visitor's center over in Drummond on Monday where we're having the classes." I hesitated. "After everything you've been through, the workshops might help take your mind off things."

Laura picked up the tray again. Her quilting enthusiasm was gone. "I hope so," she said. "You have no idea what it's been like." She climbed the stairs and, when she got to the top, knocked on a door. It opened, and Laura disappeared inside.

"Poor woman's off to console a fiancé who's lost the gal who did everything for him," I said. "What do you want to bet that Rebecca wasn't crafty?"

"We don't know, do we?" Catherine observed. "Maybe she was."

CHAPTER EIGHT

As soon as I left the Inn and was back in my car, I threw my purse on top of the basket of quilting kits and called Stuart. I wanted to know what had happened with Officer Nolan.

I was just about to hang up when he answered.

"Val." He'd recognized my number. "Where are you?" He didn't ask why I called.

"I'm driving back from the Inn, on my way home," I said. "Why?"

"Listen. I'm down at the Agapi. Can you drop by?" Stuart sounded tired and serious. "There's something I need to tell you." I heard voices in the background. Stuart paused to say hello to someone. "You were right."

I loved being told I was right. It didn't happen often enough. "I'll be there in a minute. What's this about?"

"I'll tell you when you get here." Stuart was curt. "I know what you like for lunch. I'll have it ready."

The Agapi restaurant was a block down Front Street from our store. It was the oldest, the best, and the only restaurant in Gasper's Cove. From time to time, there were rumors about someone opening another place to eat, but those plans never went anywhere. I don't think the locals felt they needed anywhere but the Agapi. The food was that good. And besides, Nick and Sophia, who had been part of the community for more than forty years, deserved our loyalty.

The menu had not changed at the Agapi since it opened. It was the same menu that would be found in any Greek restaurant in the world, from Athens to Melbourne, Australia—heavy on the lamb, garlic, lemon, and oregano, but in the Agapi's case, distinguished by Sophia's excellent, honey-sweet desserts. Her baklava was my favorite. I knew Stuart would remember to order me some.

Stuart was sitting at a booth in the window, waiting for me, when I arrived. As promised, my souvlaki and salad were already on the table. I was happy to see George Kosoulas working and to hear his laughter and banter animating the whole restaurant again. At one point, George and his dad, Nick, had clashed over updates to the menu. That had resulted in months of arguing and shouting in the kitchen until they had agreed, as good Greeks do, on a solution they could both take credit for. The Agapi, they had decided, would continue to serve what it always had, and George could experiment with Greek fusion from a food truck he'd keep well away from his father. This new arrangement worked. When he saw me, George stopped, mid-charm, at a table of lady tourists and winked.

I walked over to our booth. Stuart stood up and moved aside to let me sit close to the window, then slid back in beside me. He looked troubled and alert.

"What's up?" I asked. "And why am I right?"

Stuart leaned in, closer to me. Whatever he was about to say was not for everyone to hear.

"It was the dishwasher, not the wiring in the walls," he said quietly. "There was a new floor, linoleum. It didn't drain. That's why the water accumulated. And water is a first-class conductor."

An ugly image flashed in my mind. The dishwasher door had been opened, but the rack hadn't been pulled out.

"But where did the electricity come from?" I asked.

Stuart lifted a fork. His baklava was nearly done. Sticky walnuts were on the plate. "I pulled off the kick plate, and there it was," he said.

"What was?" I could see George was still, watching us with curiosity from across the room.

"Someone had punctured the inlet to the dishwasher feed, so water ran out and pooled on the floor. Then, this person removed the front panel to get into the ground and disabled it." My confusion must have shown on my face. Stuart stopped to explain. "The ground is the thing that keeps the electricity isolated, safe. This tampering was done by someone who knew what they were doing. That woman's death was no accident. It was a deliberate setup to kill anyone who walked over and opened the dishwasher door."

"That's what happened? That's nuts!" I squeaked. I thought I was good at entertaining unconventional ideas. I considered it part of my creativity. One of my greatest strengths. But even I had trouble processing what Stuart was suggesting. "Someone turned the dishwasher into a weapon?" A couple of teenagers at the next table snickered.

"Shh, lower your voice," Stuart said. "I know it sounds crazy, but it worked, didn't it?"

I let this sink in. "What now?" I asked.

Stuart shrugged. "I wrote a report as soon as I got back to the office. I sent it, and the pictures, to Officer Nolan. She told me she was going to call the forensic unit. They'll check it out, but I am sure I am right." George came over to the table and took our plates. Stuart waved away the offer of more coffee. "What happened yesterday was no accident. It was murder."

I remembered the outstretched hand on the linoleum floor. All she wanted was a cup. Stuart watched me. He was waiting, I realized, for me to say what he already thought.

"What if whoever set this up didn't want to kill Rebecca, that it was a mistake? Then the question is, who were they trying to kill?" I knew the answer. "Rollie or Catherine. That's who, isn't it? It's their kitchen."

"I had the same thought," Stuart said. "And I am sure Officer Nolan has, too. I mean, this was planned, it was careful, done in advance. They set it up and left, but they must have been pretty sure they knew who would get hurt."

"But why?" I asked, raising my voice. The teenagers at the next table looked at me again and whispered to each other. "To plan something like that, to do it. It's just so cold. That person would have to have a real reason. They would have to be full of anger or hate. Who would have that in them? Catherine is a librarian. Rollie doesn't have any enemies. They're innkeepers. It makes no sense."

"Innkeepers now," Stuart said. "But didn't Rollie work a long time ago in a prison?"

I was offended by what Stuart was implying. "Well, yes, but he was a therapist. His job was to help inmates deal with their issues, to get them ready for release. And that was years ago. Do you honestly think anyone would show up from his past now and do something like this?"

"I don't know," Stuart said. "Maybe it's someone who just got out."

"We have to do something," I said. "This is my cousin we're talking about. And my cousin's librarian." Rollie had had other women in his life before. Exciting women who in the end had found him too quiet. And then he'd met Catherine, a quiet woman who found him exciting. Why would trouble come for them now? It wasn't fair. "What if the RCMP don't move fast enough?" I asked.

Stuart held up his hand. "Stop right there. Officer Nolan will find the murderer. That's what she does."

"You're missing the point." I felt overwhelmed. "If somebody had a grudge against Rollie or Catherine before now, they still do." I looked out the window. The street was empty. Where had everyone gone? "I don't know who it is. But I do know they're out there, and they are not going to wait to kill again."

CHAPTER NINE

"No," Rollie said. "Definitely not. Don't bring Toby out. We don't need him."

"Yes, you do," I almost yelled into my cell phone. "Toby's big. Solid. A deterrent. He'll protect you."

"Protect me? How? By falling asleep in the doorway? By stopping the bad guys because they'll trip over him?" Rollie shot back. "I know that dog—he thinks everyone is his friend. And besides, we have Dusty."

"Dusty? "I couldn't believe this. "Dusty is a cat. An old gray cat. He can't even catch mice."

"Don't underestimate him," Rollie said." Dusty's nocturnal. He's on patrol all night. You've only seen him in the daytime when he's tired and well fed. He has a mean streak. Believe me. You try kicking him out of the bedroom at 3:00 a.m."

"Rollie!" It drove me crazy when my cousin didn't take me seriously, and he knew it. "You're not being reasonable. Why do you think I called? I'm worried. Leave the Inn. Come stay with me in town. Where there are streetlights and nosy neighbors. I'll find my key. We'll lock the doors. You're not safe out there, the two of you. Whoever messed up the dishwasher probably laid booby traps everywhere." Catherine brought me books. Rollie had given me a job when I was unemployed. Family took care of family. Didn't they understand this was my turn?

"Look, the RCMP are taking care of things," Rollie said. There was noise in the background. "Everything has been checked out. It all looks fine. They're going to send out a cruiser to come by regularly and keep an eye on the place until things settle down. If anything unusual happens, we'll contact them. I promise. Officer Nolan told us to carry on as usual. That's what we are going to do. Minus a dishwasher, of course, but that's temporary."

Rollie was as stubborn as I was. We both knew that. "What am I supposed to do?" I asked him. "I can't sit around."

"When has that ever happened?" Rollie responded. "Don't you have workshops starting tomorrow? Concentrate on that. If there is any news, you'll be the first to know."

He hung up.

I spent the rest of Sunday working on my version of Catherine's table runner. I needed the distraction. There had to be some way that I could protect Rollie and Catherine, but I couldn't figure out what it was. To calm myself, I focused on sewing. I found a small blanket stitch on my machine, put a tear-away stabilizer under the blue background fabric, and worked my way around each wave, whale tail, and boat. As always, the predictable movement of the needle, as it stepped carefully around the shapes, soothed me. I didn't know how, but creating something always seemed to lift the worries and tension from my soul and take them away. I wasn't sure where my life would be if I didn't sew.

By Monday morning, my sample was finished. By 7:00, I was at the visitor's center. When I arrived, Big Bob was already there, arranging chairs in a circle around one of the tables. I was surprised to see Gail Purves was helping him, a whisper of a smile on her bright red lips. A true eccentric, particularly a cheerful one, was impossible to resist.

I noticed four small tufts of wool roving had been set up on the table, one for each student, beside a gorgeous array of mittens Bob had laid out in pairs, next to balls of green, ocher, and woody-brown wool yarn.

Bob beamed when he saw me inspecting his display. He picked up some of the roving and pulled off a strand.

"We'll start by making the thrums. Like this," he explained, as he smoothed the roving into a piece about three inches long and brought the two ends to the middle. "You twist it to work the fibers together," he demonstrated, expertly twirling the two ends of the roving until they became one strand. "We'll get the thrums ready before we start knitting. It'll be a great little icebreaker."

I relaxed. The students would have fun with Bob. This first workshop would work out. I picked up a pair of the beautifully made mittens and admired the contrast between the natural yarn colors and the bird's-eye pattern made when the roving was knitted into a stitch. I put my hand inside one of the mitts and felt the deep insulation the roving provided. With wear, I knew the fuzzy wool would pack down, molding to the hand that wore this mitt, wrapping it in nature's best insulation.

"These are wonderful," I said. "How long have you been knitting?"

"Quite a while. Nana taught me." Bob said, adding a pair of knitted slippers to the display on the table. "It was something we started to do together when I went out to visit her at Seaview Manor. Like a lot of traditional crafts, these mitts are another example of an ingenious response to an environmental problem. They appealed to the inventor in me."

This made sense to me. Bob's inventions were legendary. He'd spent one winter trying to develop a system of bells to teach cats the alphabet, which predictably failed, and another developing a jam-making pot lid with a built-in thermometer, patent pending. I wondered if a stable career as a knitting teacher was just what he needed. I was sure I could sell hundreds of these mitts in the Co-op.

But before I could make a business proposal, Gail interrupted.

"What's this?" she asked, waving a sheaf of papers in Bob's face. "A petition? This is a nonpolitical space." She stretched out an arm, adjusted her glasses, and started to read. "*Be a voice for the Endangered Lichen of Nova Scotia?*" She looked at Bob. "Is this a joke? What does lichen have to do with mitts?"

Bob picked up two hand-wound balls of spikey wool, one in each of his large hands. "In my case, everything. I have a long-standing interest in natural dyes. Wool, it turns out, is a perfect medium. I dyed this yarn myself, using only found lichen."

Gail raised an eyebrow. "Found lichen?"

"Lichen left on the ground, not harvested," Bob explained. "It would be a violation of the ecosystem to strip it from the trees when it's still growing." He gently pulled his petition from Gail's hand and laid it reverently on the table. He reached into his knitted vest, extracted a fountain pen, and placed it carefully beside the petition. "People underestimate lichen," he said. "All the time."

Gail and I looked at each other. This was true. Bob settled in. It was clear that lichen advocacy mattered to him as much as his knitting.

"Human beings could learn a lot from lichen," he explained. "As a species, its whole existence is a story of interdependence and service. A model for the rest of us."

"Really?" I asked. I thought of the flakes of green that grew on the shady side of the trunks of the red maples in my backyard. "How's that?"

"Lichen exists only in synchrony with another organism—in this case, algae. Lichen gives insects a place to live, it breaks down surfaces so other plants can take root, it supplies birds with material for their nests." Bob sat down in a chair, put his hands behind his head, and looked up at the acoustic tile ceiling. He seemed overcome by the magnificent contributions of the lichen life cycle. "You know, scientists are researching it. Nova Scotia lichen is unique." His eyes were wide, reverent.

"For the dyes?" I asked, trying to catch up with this conversation.

"That for sure," Bob said. "Lichen has found its place in history, at this moment in time." He leaned forward and put his large hands on his knees. "Do you know that our local lichen produces more than five hundred chemicals not found anywhere else in the known universe? Nowhere else. Think that one through."

I thought of the trees in my backyard and the gray-green scales I had planned on scraping off. I'd leave it alone now.

Gail sighed. "So, that's what this is?" she asked, tapping her finger on the papers on the table. "A 'Save the Lichen' petition? I guess that's harmless, but don't"—she glared at Bob—"make this in any way a political event. Got that?"

"This is bigger than politics," Bob said to reassure her. "I have support from across the spectrum." I looked over his shoulder and read the names he had collected so far. It looked to me to be a resident list from Seaview Manor, plus the signatures of Larry Beal the algae blimp man (no surprise there), Sylvie, Bob's brother, and his sister-in-law. I picked up the pen and added my name. I felt guilty for my lichen ignorance.

"The environment thanks you," Bob said to me. He tried to hand the pen to Gail, but she waved it away. "Sometimes, it's the things you take for granted that matter most. That's what the lichen is trying to tell us."

CHAPTER TEN

I stayed for the first half hour of Bob's workshop. The students seemed delighted to be there. They laughed and chatted as they twisted wool roving, chose hand-dyed yarn for their mitts, and let themselves be charmed by Bob's enthusiasm, blond beard, and clear blue eyes.

Every one of the women was from out of province. All had signed up for the week online. In addition to Laura Sanders, who came in another fashionably creased, black-linen ensemble, there was Jane from Maine, who took copious notes and, when I said she looked like a teacher, didn't correct me; and two sisters from Alberta, Bobby and Poppy, who seemed to have come down east to giggle.

It was clear Bob was born to teach.

There wasn't a question he couldn't answer, a mistake he couldn't fix, or a tentative spirit he couldn't reassure. Satisfied that the first of our workshops was in good hands, I decided that I needed to go home and work on my own session for Wednesday. My sample had turned out well, but only because of Catherine's meticulous instructions. I wanted to go over her classroom advice again, particularly the part about staying on track to "allow time for socializing in the class, making mistakes, and needing to rip out." I hoped that if I could draw on my teaching experience and kept to her plan, the students would enjoy my workshop as much as Bob's.

On the way back to Gasper's, I decided to make a detour to Sylvie's house. Her wreath workshop was the next day. I wanted to make sure she had everything she needed. However, when I arrived at her bungalow, her van wasn't in the driveway. Only Dawn Nolan's truck and a smaller car I recognized were.

Noah Dixon was standing beside the car, writing something in a tattered spiral-bound notebook. When he looked up and saw me, he slapped the notebook closed and smiled.

I parked and walked over to him. Noah was a young reporter for the *Lighthouse Online* and a surfing friend of my youngest, Paul. I liked to think he was also a friend of mine. Every time I saw Noah, I felt younger and closer to my own son.

"Hey, Val," he said. "What's happening?"

This greeting always baffled me. What's happening is that we are talking, I always wanted to say, but this time, as always, I let it pass.

"I'm looking for Sylvie," I said. "Is she not in?"

"You just missed her, something about the kids."

I looked at Dawn's truck and then back at the house. "Were you here on official news business?" I asked. "Interviewing the RCMP?"

"No way," Noah laughed. "Dawn plays by the book. If there is anything to be said, it has to go through official channels down at the detachment. No, I was talking to her about a private project I have going on. A book."

"A book?" I asked, impressed. I had never known anyone who had written a book. "I didn't know you were doing that. Don't you already have a job? What's the book about?"

"Couple of questions there," Noah laughed. "Yes, I have a job, for the time being. You've heard we've been bought, though; a lot of the smaller papers have. I was at a meeting last week up at the Inn; East-West is taking over. They're going to be supplying 'standardized editorial content,' whatever that means. There's going to be less real reporting to do. It made me think this might be a good time to start writing for myself. I got the idea for a book from Wade."

"Wade? About sports? Hockey? Like what he's taken the summer off to do with the Maple Leafs?" I asked. Wade had been a hockey star in high school and almost a pro before he joined the RCMP. Was there a book there?

Noah shook his head. "No, nothing like that. It was his award that got me thinking."

Ah, the award. How could I forget? Wade's award, one the RCMP had given to him for heading the detachment with the country's best crime-to-solve ratio, had caused a lot of trouble at the time. "You're writing about Wade's career in law enforcement?" I asked. I couldn't see that it would be a very long book. If Wade had solved any crimes, it seemed to me most of it had been done by accident or with the help of members of the community, like me.

"Not likely," Noah said. "It was the *idea* of solving crimes that got me. It made me wonder about unsolved crimes. I started to dig around. One thing led to another. Canada has more than its share of unsolved mysteries. Did you know that? Maybe because we're such a big empty country, it makes it easy for criminals to hide out. I don't know. That's what I want to find out."

"Interesting," I said. "Like what crimes? Is that why you wanted to talk to Officer Nolan?"

"Partially, but mainly I wanted to talk to her about the war. She's got an interest in it. I figured I'd start the book by putting the theme in a historical context. I wanted to ask her about Werner von Janowski."

"Werner who?"

"He was a spy, a double agent. In 1942, a German U-boat dropped him ashore on the Gaspé Peninsula of Quebec. He was captured almost right away. A hotel clerk noticed he was trying to pay for his room with old prewar bills, if you can believe anything that dumb. Anyway, to get out of trouble, he agreed to spy for us instead. I wanted to ask Dawn if she knew of anyone else who might have come ashore, specifically around here. One of the fishermen told me an old story, about a German radio and some clothes some of the men found buried in a suitcase not far from the look-off. It got me thinking. Did someone else come through here? I thought she might know."

"Did she?" I asked.

"Possibly." Noah was evasive. "That's in the past, but it would be interesting to know. The more recent stories are just as crazy. I have so much to work with. The Great Toonie Heist of 1996. Remember that one? A million and a half two-dollar coins disappeared. Then, there's the Assiniboine Bandit, the guy who was supposed to take a huge haul of cash out west on the train but never arrived. And my personal favorite, the Skylight Caper. The thieves dropped down out of the roof at the Montreal Museum of Fine Arts and took off with paintings, old masters. In over fifty years, only two were ever found, and no one was ever caught. I could keep going. It's like disappearing is a national theme."

I felt all my worry return. Disappearing? What if they didn't catch who was responsible for Rebecca's death? What if Catherine and Rollie were never safe? And why were they targeted? "You heard about what happened at the Inn?" I asked Noah. "What you're saying is, there are many crimes that they never solve."

Noah must have seen the anxiety in my face. He tried to backtrack. "Sometimes that's true, but not often." He stopped and eyed me. "You don't know anything about that accident at the Inn, do you? Off the record?"

For a moment, I considered sharing the little I knew about Rebecca's history or the fact her death was not an accident with Noah, but I stopped myself. As far as I knew, only the RCMP, Stuart, Rollie, Catherine, and I knew that. I also knew, from past mistakes, that the Royal Canadian Mounted Police liked to release their own news. "No," I lied, counting on Noah to assume that the mother of a friend would always tell the truth. "If I hear anything, I will let you know." This was also a lie.

My phone buzzed in my pocket. I looked at it before Noah could ask me another question.

It was Darlene.

Can you come over? Right now?

"Excuse me," I said to Noah. I walked back to my car.

Why?

I tapped back.

What's wrong?

Sophia Kosoulas came to see me. She wanted to talk. You're not going to believe it.

I looked up at Noah. "Good luck with the book," I called out. "Got to go."

On my way.

I texted back.
George's mother had been to see Darlene?
What about? And why now?

CHAPTER ELEVEN

I was across the causeway and in Darlene's kitchen in ten minutes. I knew the protocol. Darlene wouldn't talk until she had a cup of tea in front of her. While we waited for the kettle to boil, I decided to count all the cat bowls on the floor. One, I noticed, had the power bill carefully laid on top.

"Funny place to keep your mail," I said.

Darlene laughed. "Oh, that's Patches," she said, referring to her calico cat. "When she finishes eating, she always covers the bowl with whatever she can find. Mail, a potholder, a sock. She learned it from Mavis."

"Mavis?" I asked. A straggly veteran of the streets, old Mavis had ended her days safe, warm, and loved in this house.

Darlene wiped away a tear. Although long gone from this earth, Mavis would always be with my cousin in her heart. "Poor old Mavis had to guard her food most of her life," Darlene explained. "Patches was one of her kittens. She must have watched her mother cover her food, so she does it herself now, even though she doesn't have to, even though she doesn't know why. Imprinted in her memory, I guess."

"That's sweet," I said. "Sad, but sweet." I had a sense Darlene was avoiding the real reason she had called. "Tell me what Sophia said."

Darlene turned off the kettle and poured the hot water into the pot. She brought it to the table with two mugs and the milk. We were both trying to drink tea these days without sugar. We both missed it. Darlene sat down but didn't settle. "Look. I know what you went through up at the Inn. That was serious, and this is ... I don't know what this is, but not serious. But I have no one else to talk to."

"Darlene, I'm here. Start at the beginning and tell me what this is about."

"Okay. Last week, when I was at the Agapi, Sophia came to the table and asked me if she could come by sometime and talk." Darlene examined the gel nails that encircled her cup. "I said, sure. The poor woman has been through a lot these last months. You know, with the food-fusion fight, George's souvlaki tacos, the grape-leaf spring rolls, his dad losing his mind over it."

"Yes, but that's been settled, hasn't it?" I said. "George has the summer to drive around in the food truck and serve what he wants. So, what's the problem?"

Darlene leaned forward. "Sophia told me this in confidence. But I can tell you. You're my cousin."

I understood. In Gasper's Cove, telling your relatives didn't count in secret-keeping. "I won't tell a soul," I promised. Unless, of course, we were related.

"Alright then." Darlene was reassured. "Here's the thing. The Agapi is Nick and Sophia's whole life. Nick's dad was on a Greek ship that carried coal from Cape Breton to New England during the war. When he went back to Greece, he told his family about Nova Scotia, how beautiful it was. That's why Nick and Sophia ended up here. It was a dream for them. The plan all along was that when Nick and Sophia retired, George would take over the restaurant. But the fight about the soy sauce in the tzatziki got Sophia thinking that maybe the food truck is just the beginning."

"It's just a converted milk truck," I pointed out. "No reason to panic."

"That's what I told her," Darlene paused. She got up and returned to the table with a round tin. She snapped off the lid. Lemon squares. I took one. "But Sophia just looked at me and said, 'Trucks have wheels. It's a sign.' But that's not all."

"What do you mean?"

"Around the same time George and Nick started fighting, Sophia went to the doctor and had some tests." She saw the concern on my face and waved it aside. "It turned out to be fine, but for two weeks, before the results came back, Sophia thought she was going to die, and her only son was going to drive away. She told me if George left here, it would be like everything she and Nick worked for never existed."

I took another lemon square. "George would never leave," I said. "He belongs here." I couldn't imagine Gasper's Cove without George Kosoulas. That man was his own power source. For as long as I had known him, all the way back to high school, George had had the kind of energy that lifted up everyone around him. In those days, whenever we had a party, the first person we invited was George. We couldn't have a good time without him. Maybe that's how his mother felt; maybe that's what she was afraid of losing. When my three children had left the city they grew up in, I had returned to the island and surrounded myself with the rest of my family. Sophia didn't have that option. In this country, George and Nick were all she had.

"I tried to tell her he'd never go, but she didn't believe me," Darlene said. "She's afraid there's nothing to keep him here because he's single, no ties. I mean, there was that woman he married from Ottawa, but she didn't last long, did she? Don't you remember?"

"How could I forget?" I nearly choked on my square. "Didn't George meet her at some resort? A whirlwind thing, wasn't it? How long was she here before she bailed? A week?"

"Not even," Darlene said. "The story is that the Foodmart did it. The new wife went in for smoked salmon and had to wait forty minutes in line because the cashier was giving a blow-by-blow description of her hysterectomy to the next lady in the line." Darlene laughed so hard, she had to put down her tea. "I heard from people who were there that she stormed out of the store, but as soon as she was outside, a seagull flew by and pooped on her head."

"That would send you back to Ontario," I admitted. "If you're not used to it. But since then, hasn't George always had some girl going? Especially in the summer, when the tourists are in?"

The expression on Darlene's face changed. I knew that we were finally going to talk about what was really on her mind.

"That's the thing," she said. "The real reason Sophia wanted to talk. She claims that every woman George dates looks like me." Darlene waited for the significance of this statement to sink in. "You know we went around together in school. She thinks he never got over me."

One of Darlene's cats stalked through the kitchen, paused at the empty bowl, and continued on its way. I leaned back in my chair. Was this possible?

I had to admit, there was some evidence it was. Now I thought about it, there were always more olives in Darlene's Greek salads than in mine. And although I hadn't measured, I was also sure that George put the larger portions of baklava on her plate. I also remembered the time last winter when I had seen George move Darlene's coat from where it had been hanging near the door of the restaurant to the hook over the heater. Those were all sure signs a man cared.

Sophia might be right.

"How do you feel about this?" I asked.

"To tell you the truth, at first I was kind of insulted. Like, how could someone love me for over twenty years and I wouldn't notice?" Darlene said. "How dumb would I be?"

"Forget that," I said. "What's more important is, how do you feel about this? About George. After all this time?"

"That's it, isn't it?" Another cat jumped up on Darlene's lap, and she reached down to stroke it. "Time. I've been thinking. You know what I decided?"

"No. Tell me."

"I've been married three times. None of them were the best choices, we both know that. But what if ..." The cat jumped on the table and tapped one of the lemon squares with a delicate nose. "What if there are some guys that when you're forty-five you realize you should have grabbed when you were twenty-five? But you didn't, because you weren't as smart then as you are now?" Darlene looked at me, the question large in her eyes. "Do you know what I mean?"

I had an image of a man sitting on my front steps. Of a man throwing a ball for a dog in a schoolyard.

"I think I know what you mean," I told her. "But what does Sophia expect you to do about it?

"That's the crazy part," Darlene said, lowering the cat to the floor and then reaching for the teapot. "Sophia has a plan."

I wasn't surprised that the part of Sophia's plan that caught Darlene's attention was the dressing up.

"She says we need a dance," Darlene explained. "She says she remembers George getting ready for dances when we were dating in school. How excited he was. How the whole house reeked of cologne. So, she came up with the idea that if she could get us together at a dance, maybe George wouldn't drive his food truck away down the highway."

I could understand Sophia's thinking. Mothers had to work with what they had. But a dance? Darlene and George were now middle-aged. Where did Sophia think she was going to find a dance? And how was she going to get them to it, anyway?

Darlene watched my face as I tried to figure this out. "I told you it was a crazy idea," she said. "Sophia has this whole scheme in her head. Music, she says, to set the mood. Low lights. She may have used the words 'sock hop.' She was so into it, I didn't have the heart to tell her it was a dumb idea."

"But a dance?" I asked. "Where?"

"Oh, she's found one," Darlene said. "Guess."

"The Chamber of Commerce?" I asked. That might be age-appropriate.

Darlene shook her head. "Not going to be another one of those until the fall."

"A wedding?" I suggested. I looked at the clock on Darlene's wall. It was shaped like a black cat, its eyes rotating with the seconds, its tail swaying with the minutes, almost as if it could hear dance music now.

"Keep trying," Darlene said.

"The Legion? The yacht club?" Gasper's Cove was small. The options were limited.

"No." Darlene shook her head. "Hold onto your hat: Seaview Manor. Tea and Tango—the seniors have it one night a month. Stuart gave her the idea. He does the music and says there are never enough men. Sophia figures she can pressure George to go with Stuart and be nice to the old ladies."

I processed this. I was most interested to hear that Stuart Campbell had a secret life as a DJ I didn't know about. But I had a question.

"What's the reason that you would be there?" I asked. "What's Sophia's angle on that one?"

"She's got that covered, too. My grandmother lives there, so the story would be that I am visiting her. Simple as that."

"You're not going to do it, are you?" I asked Darlene. "Sneak up on your old high school boyfriend at a seniors' dance? Because his mother wants you to?"

"You know, I think I will." Darlene held up her hand before I could protest. "An excuse to see my grandmother. A chance to get all done up." Her face brightened with a sly smile. "I can tango, you know."

Yes, I knew that. She was good. I gave up. "What are you going to wear?" I asked.

"That dress you said was not suitable for a deputy mayor to wear to an official event."

I knew the one. It had been hard to tell what was lower, the front or the back. "What about it?"

"It needs alterations, maybe take in a seam or two. You know, tango it up." She had another thought. "And if you run into George, maybe mention I'll be at a dance at the manor, gauge his reaction."

"Are you serious?" The cat's tail hung over the edge of the table, reminding me of the clock on the wall. It was time I went to work. I stood up and tried to think of a snappy exit line.

"Okay, I'll do it," I said. "I'll take in your dress. I'll do my best to find out if George still has romantic feelings for you. But this is it. Absolutely, definitely, the last time I get involved in any of your schemes."

Darlene and the cat both smiled at me.

We all knew that wasn't true.

CHAPTER TWELVE

All evening, while I worked on preparations for my table-runner class, I thought about Darlene. I understood Sophia's need to have her son happy and home. But I wasn't so sure if Sophia appreciated the hope she might have unleashed. I didn't know if she understood Darlene.

I did.

My cousin had been single for a long time. But unlike me, she had never quite settled into it. Despite her history of matrimonial disasters, and even though she knew better, Darlene had remained a romantic. She was a woman built to have someone to talk to every morning at breakfast and every night after dinner. All the cats in the world wouldn't change that. She had spent years trying to make the wrong men into the right ones. I had tried in the past to protect her. I had to do it again. Before Darlene went off tangoing at Seaview Manor in a newly altered dress, I had to find out if George had any interest.

How was I going to do that?

Halfway through my morning shift at the store, I had my answer.

It would be takeout Greek fusion for lunch.

I arrived back at the visitor's center before noon. Two food trucks were parked next to the tables on the edge of the water. The old ferry, *Maritime Mary,* nicknamed *The Mary,* bobbed nearby. It was a beautiful day. It occurred to me that Gail's suggestion that the workshop participants eat outside had been a good one.

One of the trucks was George's. The other, a familiar fish-and-chip wagon, was "Judd the Spud's." Unsure of exactly how I was going to approach George, I decided to stop and chat with Sammy Judd first. I walked over and tapped on the truck's small window.

I was surprised when a stranger turned around.

"Opening in a few," the large man said. Sammy Judd was small, neat, and quick. This person had a ponytail held back in a hairnet, muscular arms covered in tattoos, and blue letters engraved in the skin above each knuckle.

"Okay, sorry," I said. "Where's Sammy?"

"Recovering from a hip replacement." The new cook lowered a worn basket of hand-cut potatoes into rolling oil.

"I'm Kurt Gordon," he tossed back over his shoulder. "Taking over for the summer. A working vacation. It's a nice place to visit. I get paid to cruise around." Kurt's teeth smiled. His eyes did not.

I wanted to know more; in Gasper's Cove, we always did. I opened my mouth to start asking the usual questions. Had Kurt been here before? Did he have family in the area? What did he think of the weather? But I stopped. This man was civil, but not friendly.

"Okay, then," I said. "Good, great. Enjoy yourself." I wondered if he would. I waited for a response and got none. "Talk to you later," I added, hopefully.

The big man grunted. I moved on.

George was happier to see me. "Nice day. Can I get you something?"

"Japanese dolmades," I said. "Salad on the side." Across the parking lot, the door to the center opened. Bob and his students drifted out. I watched them, awkwardly unable to think of what to say to George. The last time I'd seen him had been at the Inn. From the look on his face, I saw he was thinking the same thing, maybe seeing the same image of the floor of that kitchen. Neither of us wanted to talk about it. I broke the silence. I had a job to do.

"Listen, I was over at Darlene's," I started. George was paying close attention. I would have to tell this to Darlene. "The folks at Seaview Manor are having a dance. They do it every month; Stuart does the music. We were thinking of getting a few people together to go. The seniors would like the company. You interested?"

I watched George's face for clues of interest. I knew my story sounded lame, but it was the best I could do.

"Sure," George said slowly. I saw amusement in his face and something else. Maybe a trace of suspicion. "Why not? When is it?"

"Friday?"

"I have it off this week. Sure, I'll go. My mom mentioned it, too. Several times. I had no idea these dances were a thing." George winked at me. I had a sudden sense that Darlene had met her match, or maybe found it. "Stuart know you're going?" George asked. I was being out maneuvered, and we both knew it.

I changed the subject. I pointed over to the fish-and-chips truck. "See you got a new competitor here," I said. "How's that going?"

George shrugged. "Nice enough guy. Keeps to himself. When Sammy's turn came up at the hospital and he knew he'd be laid up, he put out the word for someone to take over for awhile. This guy showed up."

"From where?" I asked. I didn't know why this mattered to me.

"Somewhere in central Canada," George said. "Not sure where. He knows his potatoes, but he doesn't know fish. Don't tell Sam, but I think he's using cod. Frozen."

I shuddered. Sammy Judd was a fresh halibut man.

Bob's students ambled over. Jane from Maine knitted while she walked. The twins made a beeline for fish-and-chips. Laura Sanders joined me at George's window. I moved aside to make room for her, collected my lunch, and walked over to Bob.

"How's it going?" I asked him.

"Great, I'd say. We got the ribbing all done and the thrums started to knit in. We'll be right up past the thumb opening by the end of the day." Bob looked pleased with himself. "I wasn't sure I'd like teaching, but I do. A lot. And I've got orders for more of my wool." He stopped, thoughtful. "You know, after all the things I've tried, I think my yarn could be the one that turns into a real business. Who would have thought?"

"Me," I said. "The colors are beautiful. The lichen-dye angle is pretty unique. It's a mass-produced world out there.

People are looking for the real thing. Forage all the lichen you can, and whatever yarn you make, I'll sell it at the Co-op."

"Deal," he said. Jane came up to stand behind Bob and coughed. She held up her knitting. "My thrums," she said, holding up the beginning of a mitt. "Am I doing this right?" I could see the first row of tiny white Vs on the right of the stockinette, the tufts of wool roving like little cotton balls, woven into the bumps of the purl inside.

Bob took the knitting and four needles from her and studied it seriously. "You might want to tighten it up just a tad," he said, "but I'd say you got it. Good for you."

Jane beamed and started to ask another question, this one very specific, about tension. I stepped back to let the teacher and student confer and looked around. Over at one of the picnic tables, the twins, Bobby and Poppy, were attacking massive pieces of battered fish with tiny wooden forks. Laura Sanders, her soft leather slides crunching on the gravel as she walked, went over to join them, a paper plate with two of George's souvlaki tacos in her manicured hands.

There was something different about Laura today. The jewelry and black linen were the same. Her meticulously streaked hair and aesthetician-shaped brows were perfect, just like they had been the day I met her. But something had changed or was missing.

Then, it hit me.

Although Laura's outside was still carefully put together, something underneath had been untied. I watched as she laid her overflowing plate down on the picnic table, smiled at the twins, and giggled.

I knew what it was.

Laura Sanders, fiancée of a man whose right-hand gal had been found dead not that long ago, today looked lighter, relaxed.

She popped open a ginger ale and drank it from the can. One of the twins said something funny, and she sputtered. I knew what was different.

This Laura Sanders was happy.

CHAPTER THIRTEEN

I was on my way to talk to the women from the workshop when Gail Purves walked up and held a small screen in front of my face.

"When were you going to mention this?" she demanded. "I knew something was up."

I took the phone from her and read:

Suspicious Death at Local Bed-and-Breakfast

The RCMP has confirmed in a press release that Ms. Rebecca Coates, an event organizer employed by East-West Media, was found dead Friday morning in the kitchen of the Bluenose Inn on the north shore of Gasper's Island. When asked for more details, specifically to confirm rumors in the community that foul play was involved in the incident, Officer Dawn Nolan would only say that the RCMP is "proceeding with a murder investigation. No further comment is available at this time."

> East-West Media is a countrywide publishing and broadcasting conglomerate that has recently acquired the *Lighthouse Online* as part of a strategy to expand its Atlantic Canadian holdings.
>
> East-West Company president Parker Wallace said in a statement, "Rebecca was with me from the start. She shared my vision for raising the standard of news coverage across all corners of this great country. It saddens me to know she won't be here to see our continued success. She will not be easy to replace."
>
> When interviewed, Catherine Walker and Rollie Rankin, co-owners of the Bluenose Inn, said they "are devastated" and doing everything they can to "help the RCMP." Rankin also said, "All we can think of is her family and friends. I don't understand it. That was a new dishwasher."
>
> The *Lighthouse* will continue to follow and report on the ongoing investigation into the death of Ms. Coates.

"I knew there was something fishy about these workshops." Gail's voice was so loud that Bobby, Poppy, and Laura looked up from their picnic table. I saw that all three had phones in their hands. Poppy stood up and came over to me, her sister and Laura close behind.

"This is why you moved us here to the visitor's center, isn't it?" she asked. "The Inn is the scene of a crime. A murder." The revelation didn't seem to upset her. "And this lady here," she gestured to Laura, "is still staying there."

"True," Laura said. She didn't seem to mind the attention at all. "Parker, that's my fiancé, has gone to play Highland Links. But I stayed here for this." She spread her arms wide, taking in a seagull eating a chip that had fallen on the gravel, Jane counting stitches with a steel knitting needle in her teeth, and *Mary* the ferry bumping her weary hull against the timbers of the dock. "So worth it."

Beside her, Poppy evaluated me, a plan forming in her eyes. "You are having another one of these retreats, aren't you?" she asked me. "Next month. Isn't that one going to be at the Inn?"

"I suppose so," I said. August seemed far away, as distant as the life I had been living this time last week. I watched Gail stalk off back to the center. It was unlikely my retreats would be welcome here again.

"Boy oh boy. Everyone will want to go to that one," Bobby said. "I'll bet there's a waiting list now. It's like Agatha Christie." She looked at her phone and scrolled to the last line in the news story. "Death by dishwasher," she said, raising her eyebrows at her sister.

Poppy knew what her twin was thinking. "We have another sister at home," she explained. "Wait till she hears about this. If we pay her registration now do you think you can fit her in for the next session? She'd be dying to get here."

I waited until Bob led his students back into the center for the rest of the day before I left. My head was spinning. The twins had texted their sister in Calgary—her name was Holly—and signed her up for the August workshops. This act, small as it was, overwhelmed and frightened me. It was hard to accept that trouble was an attraction. It was only when I got home and saw Toby that I felt safe. I let him out into the backyard, made myself tea, and went outside and sat down on the top step of the deck to think.

Oblivious to the world outside his yard, Toby loped around. I couldn't lead Toby's life, and I wished I could. The story in the *Lighthouse* had said it all: It was all up to the RCMP. Keeping Rollie and Catherine safe was not my job. There was nothing I could contribute, nothing I could do. No one wanted my help, my involvement, or my interference. From now, on I needed to focus on my own projects, and I put everything else out of my mind.

A blue jay flew into the yard. Toby looked up and barked, protecting me. I stood up to take my cup into the house, then I stopped, my hand on the handle of the back door.

What if Stuart was right and someone from Rollie's past had come into the area to find him?

Who would know who that was?

I knew someone.

I had an ex-con on staff.

Tomorrow, I would be at Rankin's General before it opened.

"You never bring me coffee." Duck stopped pushing his broom and looked at me warily. "What's up?"

I had thought I could employ all my crafty skills to ease into this conversation. That wasn't going to happen. I decided to try a sideways entry.

"Your family," I asked, trying to compose my features into a guileless arrangement. "How are they these days?" There was no way to make this question sound as innocent as I wanted. I knew, and Duck knew, that his family was always in trouble. They'd even made a stab, years ago, at serious crime. That had involved a counterfeiting scheme in a garage in Montreal. At the time, they had tried to use an unwitting Duck to pass off the bills. That hadn't worked out. The bills had all been printed with the same serial number. Duck had been caught and done time. Rollie had rescued him and given him a place at the store. The rest of his brothers, as far as I knew, were still circulating in and out of the prison system. Who better than a Macdonald to know if a recently released convict had a grudge against Rollie?

Duck sighed. I hadn't fooled him. "Which ones do you want to know about? The ones who are in jail? The ones who just got out? Or the ones that haven't been caught yet?"

"All of them," I answered. "I lose track."

"I don't know why this matters, but here goes," Duck said. "My older brothers are semiretired. Maybe some illegal lobster traps, that's it. The other boys, some of the cousins, they're still at it, here and there, but more minimum-security stuff. Nothing to do with me. Why do you want to know?"

"Duck, I know you're not like the rest of your family," I tried to reassure him. "They've caused you enough trouble."

"You got that right," Duck said. He leaned his broom against the wall. I saw a familiar look of hereditary doom and resignation on his Elvis Presley–handsome face. He had a right to leave his past behind. I felt bad about bringing this up. But I had a job to do. Protecting my own family.

I looked around to see if anyone could hear me. We were in the plumbing supply aisle, hardware on one side, electrical on the other. It was early in the morning, so all three aisles were empty.

"You know that woman who died at the Inn?" I asked, looking up at the old general store's pressed-metal ceiling. I didn't want to say murder, but we both knew that was what I meant.

Duck stared at me. "The Macdonalds aren't killers," he said. I had offended him.

"No, everybody knows that." I tried to wave the suggestion away. "Look, I'm wondering if maybe it was Catherine, or more likely Rollie, the killer was out to get. What do you think?"

"Rollie?" Duck picked up his broom and held it in both hands, like it was a weapon he was going to use to defend my cousin. "Nobody's got anything against Rollie. Look what he did for me. Talked to me inside, made me understand that I didn't have to go down my brothers' road. Got me this good job when I got out."

"I know, and we are lucky to have you here," I said. I felt guilty I was doing this. Rebuilding his life had been hard enough for Duck. "But I'm worried, so I have to ask. Is there someone, maybe with a history of violence, who knew Rollie from when he worked in the system as a counselor and might want to hurt him? Not someone you know, but your family might. I realize this is the last thing you want to do, ask them, but I'm just trying to ..."

Duck finished my sentence for me. "Protect Rollie. I get it." His grip on the broom handle was so tight, his knuckles were white. "I know which brother to ask. I'll get in touch with him. He owes me. If there's a guy going after Rollie, I'll find out. But"—he looked at me hard—"if I get a name, you got to promise me two things."

"Sure, anything," I said.

"One, you take the information straight to the RCMP, and two, you back off." I wasn't sure why Duck felt he had to say this, but I nodded anyway. "Don't you tell anyone where you got the information. You got that? This can't be traced back to me or my brothers. If they think that could happen, they'll never talk."

"Deal," I said. "Just see what you can find out."

"Oh, I will," Duck said. "Count on it. If it wasn't for the Rankins, I don't know where I'd be."

As I watched Duck push his broom into aisle three, boat supplies, I felt better. Rollie wouldn't let me send Toby out to the Inn to protect him, but this I could do. Now, all I had to do was wait.

My phone beeped. I had a message from Sylvie. Her class was going well. I'd do my workshop tomorrow, then my first retreat would be done. Relieved, I walked to the front of the store. Darlene's mother, Colleen, was at the counter.

"That order of hardware came in," she said when she saw me. "You want to bag it, or should I do it?"

"I'll take care of it," I said. "I'll help you get caught up here."

"Appreciate it," Colleen said, then hesitated. "You know what you've done don't you?" she asked.

I stopped. Had Colleen heard my conversation with Duck? I busied myself rearranging the Nova Scotia flags we kept in a small pail next to the counter, avoiding her eyes. "What do you mean?" I asked. I thought I knew. Colleen wouldn't approve of me upsetting Duck, and even less if she knew I had tried to activate the Macdonald criminal network.

"You've got them all stirred up," Colleen said. "I was up to see my mom, and they were in full swing."

"Who?" I asked.

"The ladies' league of never-retired matchmakers, Seaview Manor division." Colleen poked me in the ribs. "When I got there, Sophia had just left. My mom and her friends were having a grand old time putting two and two together. You and Darlene at Tea and Tango. The same dance where Stuart Campbell will be the DJ and George will be at, too."

"Oh, come on," I said. This was crazy. That Stuart would be there was incidental. Sophia had set this in motion, not me. "The ladies should take it easy. There's nothing to it. We just thought it would be a nice thing to do."

"Ha, as if anybody's going to buy that." Colleen leaned over the counter, her weight on her elbows. She was enjoying herself. "The thing about seniors is, they were not born yesterday. My mom and her friends are ready to go. They're going to give you a hand."

"A hand?" I asked. I didn't like the sound of this. "With what?"

"Your double date," Colleen beamed at me. My heart sank. "I hear they are working on a surprise."

CHAPTER FOURTEEN

Colleen had nothing else to share with me. The more I tried to get details about what Bernadette and her friends were up to, the more evasive Colleen was, and the more she smirked.

Finally, I gave up and went off to the back of the store to unpack the hardware order. I found the cart with the order of screws at the end of the last aisle. Beside it, Colleen had placed a stapler, a roll of price tags, and the cardboard box of the small plastic bags we used to package fasteners. My job was to fill each bag with twenty screws of the same size, staple the bag shut, slap on a price tag, and peg the bags on the wall. Bagging the screws was a mindless activity, but today that was exactly what I needed. I pulled up an ancient footstool, sat down, and reached into the first box of woodworking screws. I saw they were our best sellers, the #8s. I started to sort them by length, counting out loud as I went.

"Seventeen, eighteen, or was that nineteen? Twenty?" I asked myself. Counting had never been my best thing.

“There’s an easier way to do that,” a voice whispered.

I hadn’t heard anyone come up behind me. Startled, I dropped the box of three-quarters inches. The screws rolled across the floor, some disappearing under the first row of metal shelving.

“Sorry,” the voice said. I looked up. It was Larry Beal, the man who floated a survey blimp along our coast, who coauthored a “save the lichen” petition, and who scavenged the lobster rope Sylvie used to make her wreaths. I had seen Larry in the store before but never talked to him. Most times, he scurried in, grabbed his supplies, and left, as if part of his mission was to avoid human contact. This was the closest I had ever been to him, and I looked him over. He was a man in his late fifties, his face lined, his cheeks and around his mouth covered with a short layer of stubble, like gray Velcro. He was dressed neatly, however, his plaid shirt tucked into jeans pulled tight with a heavy leather belt. Over this, he wore a multi-pocket vest unzipped. It was an outfit that looked like it had come in the mail from L.L. Bean but had been ordered in a size too large. As someone who taught fitting classes, I thought Larry Beal looked lost and small in his clothes. The collar of his shirt stood away from his neck as he crouched low, head down, and began scooping the errant screws toward me in a pile.

“I’ll help.” His voice sounded scratchy. Out of practice. “How many in each bag?”

“Twenty,” I told him.

Beal nodded and turned to the other side of the aisle. After studying the supplies, he reached over and grabbed a metal drywall spatula and paint tray.

"Counting's easier if you work by fives," he said. He dropped a handful of the screws into the trough of the tray and with the spatula deftly flicked four groups into a bag.

He made it look easy. After a moment, he handed the tray and spatula to me. "Neat trick," I said. It was. Larry stood up. "What did you come in for?" I asked him. "Anything I can help you with?"

"The usual," he said, looking toward the back of the store. "I came to fill up the propane. I got to stay on track, get the blimp up as soon as the tide's out and light's still good. Easier to get pictures of the kelp beds."

"Kelp?" I asked. "That's big seaweed. I thought you were doing government work on algae."

"Not working for the government," Larry nearly snorted. "They move too slow. I'm with a private foundation. Kelp's a kind of algae, you know. But we are most interested in the microalgae species. The kind you can't see but grows in the same area."

Sounded pretty dull, I thought. That opinion must have shown in my face.

"Food source of the future," Larry added. I detected a tone of annoyance, or maybe defiance, in his voice. The rest of the world, represented by me, didn't take algae seriously enough.

"Microalgae?" I asked, trying to keep the skepticism out of my voice. "Who's going to eat that?" I'd eaten dulse, dried red seaweed, and tried dehydrated strips of brown kelp. "Kale of the sea," Darlene called it. Seaweed might be good for you, she said, but it tasted like salty paper.

Larry took a step back. "The world's going to eat it," he explained tightly. "A hungry world. I have a question for you. How long do you think it takes to get the protein in beef? From a production point of view, field to table?"

"No idea," I said, which was true.

"Two years," Larry said. "And the same amount of protein, nutrient-dense, vegan protein can be grown in algae in less than a week." I was amazed, not the least because I had never seen Larry Beal this alive, engaged, or animated. But he was now. Over algae.

"So, that's why the foundation is mapping the coast?" I asked, trying to redeem myself. "To find out where they can harvest algae?" I strained to consider the appeal of green sludge on a plate. I tried to imagine the recipes.

"Partially. The water is warming. Look what happened to eelgrass. The kelp beds are shrinking. We're running out of time." Beal looked past me to the bags of screws on the wall, as if seeing in them his assignment, his commitment, his destiny. "I can't miss a thing," he said. "Got to be on the lookout. All the time."

I stopped what I was doing. I put a filled bag of screws down. Larry Beal and I looked at each other. In his obsession, I saw something familiar, a part of myself, in this man. And I saw an idea. It wasn't just the tangles of big kelp Larry saw or only the mist of hidden algae. This man saw everything. All along the coast. With his own eyes or through the drop cameras on the belly of a remote-controlled blimp. He was a watcher, a hoarder of details, a collector of things noticed.

I recognized him. I knew who he was.

An ally. It wouldn't hurt to ask.

"I wonder if you could do something for me?" I asked. I waited for a response, and when there was none, I continued. "Something is going on, there's someone here."

Larry's body went still, but his eyes were warm, interested. "What do you mean?" he asked.

"I'm sure you heard about that lady who died at the Inn." Larry nodded. "It looks like what they thought was an accident wasn't. But the thing that has me worried is, what if it wasn't her they were trying to kill, but my cousin Rollie or Catherine? What if the killer is still here and going to try again?" The anxiety I had been working to suppress came back, full force. "I can't sit around and wait for that to happen. And I think you can help me."

"What do you want me to do?" Larry asked. I noticed he didn't tell me I was crazy. I appreciated that.

"You've got eyes," I said. "A camera on the blimp. What if you notice something out of place? Something or someone who shouldn't be here? Does that make sense? Can you do that? And let me know?"

Larry stared at me, while he considered my proposal, as if examining it on the surface and turning it over and checking underneath for flaws. I was thankful then that he was no ordinary man.

"I understand, you're doing your best," he said, finally. "You're afraid there's someone who wants to hurt your family. I could see how that could be ... terrifying." For a quick moment, I thought I saw empathy in Larry's face, a sadness, then it was gone. "I try not to miss much. I'll tell you what—I see something, I'll let you know."

I felt relieved. I was no longer alone.

CHAPTER FIFTEEN

Sylvie's lobster-rope wreath class was finishing up when I arrived at the visitor's center.

I tip-toed in and stood at the back of the room.

"There you have it." Sylvie held up the sample. "A piece of maritime history replicated with your own hands. One continuous length of rope. One simple Turk's head knot."

Laura admired her own work. "Tricky, but once you have a system, it's not that hard," she said. Her wreath was perfect, even and symmetrical, every loop laid, intertwined, and laced exactly where it should be.

Next to her, Jane from Maine stopped lashing the cut edges of the rope together on the backside of her work and looked over, her red reading glasses low on her nose. "This knot we're using is a thousand years old. Crazy," she said. "And different colors for different fishing areas and different species. It's like a secret code."

Sylvie nodded. "I know, cool, eh? That's one of the reasons I like to use rope that's washed up on shore. It comes to us from everywhere. Sometimes, it's rough, been in the water too long, but most of the time, we can still use it. I think the texture adds character."

"We'll have to explain this when we're back in Calgary," Bobby laughed. "They're not going to believe it. Look at my rope. Yellow and black. Yellow for lobster, black for the maritime region. Poppy's got green, fishing area 35." She studied her twin's wreath more closely. One side looked lopsided. "I think you missed a loop there," she pointed out.

"Yeah, I know," Poppy said. "Not to worry. I'm going to put a nice bow on that part to cover it up."

"Good plan," Bobby said. "You could use a heart for Valentine's Day and a pumpkin for Halloween. Be very cute."

At the other end of the table, Jane rolled her eyes. Suppressing a smile, Sylvie started coiling up the unused rope, looping it back and forth from one palm to over her elbow. The class was nearly done. Leaving her to it, I went off in search of Gail.

I found the manager in her office. She didn't seem very glad to see me.

"Only one more day and I can clear out that room," she said as a greeting. "Good thing I was able to rebook the painters."

"I appreciate the space and your help," I said. I was sure this was the fourteenth time I had thanked this woman for doing her job, which was to be hospitable. "But I wanted to confirm about tomorrow. We'll be using sewing machines, and I'm bringing the irons. Do we have enough extension cords?" Years earlier, I had attended a sewing festival in Toronto. The event organizer had said there were only two things that mattered when planning a big activity: the concept and the extension cords. I'd never forgotten that.

"Done," Gail said. "And you can take them with you. I was up at the Inn at the end of last week. I might have borrowed some by mistake." Seeing the look on my face, she attempted an explanation. "I heard Rollie and Catherine were doing good business. I wanted to see for myself. Catherine was clearing out the conference room for some gathering. I helped her carry a few things out. Turns out, I brought the cords home. These things happen."

Do they? In the back of my mind, an uncomfortable feeling was pushing others aside to make its way to the front. What was it trying to tell me? I needed to be alone to figure it out.

I tripped over a wrinkle in the center's indoor/outdoor carpeting in my hurry to get out the door. I felt Gail's eyes on my back. "I have a dog to walk," I said over my shoulder. "I'll see you tomorrow. With my irons." I didn't know what else to say. My intuition had found the connection. This made so much sense. But what was I going to do with this knowledge?

I had no idea.

Toby wasn't much help.

As soon as I got home, I clipped the leash to my dog's harness, and we headed off on our usual route, up to the school and around the neighborhood.

"Toby, I'm going to lay it out for you," I said. "Tell me if this makes sense."

Toby had his nose to the ground, but I thought I saw his ears rotate backward. He was listening.

"This is what I know: A woman was killed. The RCMP are trying to find out who wanted her dead. That's their job, that's where they would start." Toby kept walking, eyes straight ahead, looking for other dogs or, even better, cats. He didn't disagree with me.

"I wanted the RCMP to watch out for Rollie and Catherine." Toby stopped and looked up at me. I had his attention. He'd heard Rollie's name. "There's a cruiser that's going to drive by the Inn every now and then. But what good is that?" Toby started walking again, thinking this over.

"I mean, if someone is out to get Rollie or Catherine, who's going to stop them if it isn't me? Us?"

Toby found a sandwich some child had dropped in the schoolyard. He swallowed it before I could stop him.

"Toby, concentrate," I said. "This is serious. I need your help. What I want to tell you is that I have decided Gail Purves could be the murderer. I can't believe I am saying it, but it's what I think."

Toby burped. I didn't think he was convinced.

"Look, she has a chip on her shoulder because of that occupancy-tax thing I don't understand. And I can't for the life of me figure out what brought her to Gasper's Cove. And now I have evidence she was at the Inn sometime before Rebecca died."

I wasn't sure if Toby heard me. His nose was under a bench near the monkey bars in the playground. The idea that children at recess might have dropped food was a revelation.

"It has to be her," I continued to the only audience I had. "Either she wanted to hurt Rollie or Catherine directly or she wanted to damage their business." The more I thought about it, the more it made sense. "She organizes events herself. She knows how important extension cords are, so she took them to sabotage their conference. Then, she rigged a fatal accident to discredit them." I thought my head would explode. One murderer, two motives. It was more than enough. Toby looked over at the field where Stuart had thrown the ball for him and sighed.

"I know what you're thinking," I said to my dog. "I should talk to Stuart. But you know what he's like. He likes specifications, not speculation. No one is going to listen to me unless I have evidence. I can't be waiting for Duck to bring me rumors from jail or for some blimp guy to notice something. I have to act. Now."

Toby sat down and stared at me. His big brown eyes were patient while he waited for me to listen to myself.

"That's it, isn't it?" I asked the dog. Toby walked over and licked my hand in support, or maybe he was looking for a treat. "I'm there with her tomorrow, teaching my class. I'll look around, talk to her, maybe get her to slip up. I'll be safe, people around me. What do you think?"

Toby walked over to a clump of dandelions and lifted a leg.

I tried not to take this personally.

CHAPTER SIXTEEN

The next day, Wednesday, was my turn.

I wanted the workshop to run well, even though I felt distracted by looking for opportunities to implicate Gail in a murder. Fortunately, Catherine had prepared carefully, and that helped anchor me. It was a well-designed project that taught several basic skills—appliqué, outline quilting, and mitered corners on French double-fold binding. The appliqué shapes, as Laura had noted, were already printed on the fusible web. That helped, too.

"All right, ladies," I began, sneaking a look at Catherine's instructions. "The first step is to fuse the web onto the fabric and then cut out the shapes. Six sailboats, six waves, and four whale tails. When that's done, we can peel off the paper."

"Make sure when you fuse the shapes to the runner fabric that you have the web right-side down," Laura added. "You don't want to fuse anything to the iron."

Jane from Maine nodded and picked up a pressing cloth. I carried on and held up a sheet of stabilizer. "Step 2, stitch the appliqués down. Put this under the fabric so the stitches don't pull up."

"Loosen your upper tension on the machine, too," Laura suggested. "Makes a nicer stitch."

"True," I agreed, "just like buttonholes."

The twins had their machines threaded. Laura went over to help them with their tension. I eyed the door of the classroom and saw Gail at the front desk, drawing something on a map for a visitor with a large-lens camera around his neck. She saw me looking at her and turned her back. I wondered if she knew I thought she was a killer. I pulled layers of thin batting and backing fabric out of my bag. I walked around the room and put one of each in front of every machine.

"Remember not to backstitch," I told the class as I circled the tables, checking on progress.

"Yes, leave the threads long so you can pull them through to the back and tie them off," Laura instructed. Jane finished her stitching, nodded, and turned her top over.

Poppy held up her runner to show me. One of the whale tails was backward. "Messed up a bit, but who's going to notice?" she asked.

"No one," her twin reassured her. "Just put a plant or a coffee cup over that part." Poppy looked at the clock, then out the window to the food trucks. "Is it time for lunch?" she asked. Doing the last sailboat had done her in.

"It is," I said. "After you eat, we can come back, safety-pin the top to the batting and the backing, and start quilting."

"I brought my free-motion foot," Laura announced. "The quilting shouldn't take long."

I hadn't planned on anyone doing free motion: That was another skill for another day. "Or you can just outline stitch around the shapes," I told the class, lifting my own table runner up in demonstration. "That's what I did in my sample."

The twins glanced at my stitching, grabbed their wallets, and headed for the door. Jane waited for Laura. She had already identified the real teacher in this class. We both had.

I reached out and touched Laura's arm as she made her way over to Jane.

"You've quilted before, haven't you?" I asked. There was more to this woman than she let on.

Laura laughed. "A bit. Here and there. YouTube."

"Well, I appreciate your help," I said. Together, Laura and I walked out of the multipurpose room and past the front desk. Gail motioned to me. "Question for you," she said. "Do you mind?"

I have questions for you, too, I thought.

"You go ahead," I said to Laura. I stopped beside Gail.

"What can I do for you?" I asked the manager, my suspect.

"I have a meeting I can't get out of," Gail said with distaste. "The council. Budget discussions. It's later this afternoon. I'll lock the door. Put up a sign. But are you going to be okay in there if I leave you alone?"

I couldn't believe my luck. It was as if the Fates had stepped in to help me, recognizing they had to. If there was evidence in this building that might implicate Gail in the death at the Inn, I'd have a better chance of finding it with her gone.

"No problem, we're good. Perfect." I tried to disguise my enthusiasm. The class would be over by three o'clock. I should have lots of time to look around.

Gail hesitated. "Lock the door when you're done?" she asked. "There are things of value in here."

"I don't doubt it," I said, thinking, *I sure hope so.* "You go. Take your time."

I had never been so impatient for four women to apply double-fold binding in my life. The quilting had gone well. Most of the class had outline-stitched around the whale tails, boats, and waves. Laura stippled her way around hers like an expert, holding the frame of her hands still as she worked.

The binding took more time. I had made several samples of how to miter the corners and was glad that I had. Jane caught on quickly, but the twins opted for square corners instead. Laura already knew what to do.

By ten after three, we were done. I had survived my first, unscheduled, retreat.

"You'll let us know?" the twins asked, as they packed up their machines. "About the waitlist for the next session? You know, the one that's going to be at the Inn? Where there was that murder? A couple of girls from our sister's work are also interested."

"I have your email addresses," I reminded them. "I'll let you know." I looked out to the parking lot. Laura and Jane were together, deep in discussion, their runners laid out on the hood of the Lexus. Laura had her arms held out at an angle and was swaying as she stood, no doubt giving Jane a parking-lot session in free-motion quilting. Next to them, the spot marked with the manager's sign was empty.

This was my chance.

I hustled the twins out the door and locked it behind them. What should I do first?

I looked at Gail's chair behind the reception desk. She'd left a light sweater draped over the back. I felt her presence.

The manager had a motive to cause trouble at the Inn, and she'd been there, so she'd had the opportunity, too. But did she have the means?

Past the sweater and the chair, I saw a closed door. I knew that behind it was the manager's private office. I would start there. I slipped behind the desk and opened the door.

I was disappointed.

Gail's office looked like no one worked there. There were some props on the desk, a combination blotter and calendar with cryptic notes on some dates, and four pens and a pencil lined up perpendicular to the edge of the desk, but that was all. I pulled on the handles of the desk drawers and was surprised they were unlocked. I'd start my search there.

The top drawer held paper clips, a short mason jar of rubber bands, and a small package of tissues. The second drawer held a Tupperware box with nothing but crumbs inside and a few packages of wooden knives and forks like the ones dispensed at the food truck for fish-and-chips. In the bottom drawer was a bag with a long zipper end to end. I unzipped it. Inside, there was a pair of very large shoes, black and red, flat, with laces that went almost down to the toes. The shoes looked too big for Gail, more like men's, but somehow familiar.

I closed the desk drawers and looked around. There was nothing personal in this room, nothing to give any hint of the person it belonged to, none of the usual photos, no dying plants on the windowsill, not even dust.

I was disappointed.

Then, I saw it. Tucked in the corner behind the door. A small wardrobe, chipboard and plastic woodgrain, the kind the municipality provided. I went over and opened it.

Inside were a pair of slip-on rain boots—duckies, we called them—and a billowing poncho with the community's logo on the chest. I pushed the hanger with the poncho aside and saw a plastic garment bag behind it. I unzipped it. There, on a wire hanger and covered with a dry cleaner's paper sleeve, was a shirt. I slipped my hand up into the hanger and pulled the shirt off. I stepped back and held it up for a closer look.

The shirt was rayon challis, a nice weight, a man's XXL, well-worn, pressed with creases along the tops of the sleeves, a cardboard dry cleaner's number safety-pinned inside the back of the neck. I turned the shirt over. On the back were words. Gold letters on black.

Purves Electrical

A Family Business Since 1952

I dropped the shirt onto the floor. I picked it up, folded it carefully, and put it into my bag.

This was it.

Gail Purves would know how to rig a dishwasher and turn it into a killing machine. It was obvious. She'd come from a family of electricians.

This rayon shirt with its custom embroidery was going straight to the RCMP—not as a clue, not as evidence, but as a solution to a crime.

And that crime was murder.

CHAPTER SEVENTEEN

Behind me, the door clicked.

I whipped around, stubbing my toe on an object on the floor near the edge of the desk. It was a bright pink hand weight. I could see "8 lbs." printed on it from where I stood. Gail walked toward me from the open doorway. She reached down and picked up the weight.

"What do you have there?" she asked, tossing the weight back and forth, hand to hand. "In the bag. Taking something?"

I froze.

What should I do? I didn't like the way Gail was looking at me. Or the ease with which she handled the weight, like a bludgeon. Like I could be her next victim.

I pulled the folded shirt out of the bag and laid it on the desk, like a distraction, or a bargaining chip I was surrendering before it could do me much good.

Gail's eyes went wide.

"Jimbo's shirt? You can't take that! What are you doing?" she demanded. I was surprised to see more pain than anger on her face.

Terrible on my feet, I grasped at straws. I resorted to all I could think of.

The truth.

"*Purves Electrical*, it's written on the back. That's got to be your family. It all makes sense. You grew up in the electrical business. That's why you have the skills to mess with the dishwasher. Who else would think of that as a way to shock Rollie or Catherine to death?"

Gail's mouth fell open. Her hand on the weight tightened. She probably couldn't believe anyone had figured her out, that she'd been caught.

I knew I was moving into deep waters, that the bottom was long gone, but I kept going. "You killed Rebecca Coates," I said, stating it as a fact. "You had no way of knowing she'd go into the kitchen before they did. You didn't mean it to be her, but that doesn't matter. You killed her."

"A dishwasher? What does that have to do with Jimbo's bowling shirt?" Gail picked up the rayon shirt and hugged it to her chest. She staggered over to a chair and sat down. "I didn't kill anybody. What gave you that idea?"

Motive, opportunity, and means, I wanted to say. Just like on Netflix. Instead, I answered her question with one of my own. I still had some details to fill in.

"Who are you, anyway? Why are you here?" I asked her. "Nobody comes from away to work a seasonal job in a small-town visitor's center. Not without some other reason. What is it?" Tell me, I almost said, what makes a murderer?

"I want to go pro," Gail sighed. "Be inducted into the Hall of Fame."

I stared at her. What? Was she telling me her ambition was to be a serial killer? This was worse than I had thought.

How many dishwashers in how many communities had she rigged? How many innocent people had she electrocuted? The eight-pound pink weight was still in her hand. Was she getting ready to strike? I pulled up a chair for myself and sat down, placing my fabric bag up high in my lap in case I needed it to deflect a blow.

"Hall of Fame?" My mouth was dry. My water bottle was in the classroom.

"The ICBA. The International Candlepin Bowling Association. Jimbo, my husband, was my coach," Gail laid a hand gently on the shirt on the desk. "My dad sponsored the team—that's why our name was on the shirt. Jimbo was a lot older than I was, but it didn't matter. We had twenty-five wonderful years. He always said I was the best. I wanted to keep going. For his sake."

For one of the first times in my life, I was speechless, then I recovered. "Candlepin? You mean bowling with those little balls and skinny pins?"

"You got it," Gail said. "It's a game that's played only in New England. New Hampshire—that's where I grew up—Maine, and Massachusetts. And only in Nova Scotia and New Brunswick here in Canada. I think there's one alley in Ohio."

"I'm missing something," I said. This was an understatement. Gail had put the pink dumbbell down on the desk. I found this reassuring. "But before I say anything else, my condolences about your husband. I'm sorry I borrowed his bowling shirt. I didn't know." This was true. Candlepin bowling was not an angle I had considered. My evaluation of Gail as a cold-blooded murderer would need to be modified. "But it still doesn't explain why you are here, or to be honest, why you don't like the Rankins."

"Alright. Here's the thing. You're not an elite athlete yourself, so you might not understand." Gail reached for the weight again and flexed it as she talked, rolling it in her right hand toward her chest, up and down. I caught sight of her wrists below the cuffs of her blouse as the tendons rose and fell with the movement. "Training costs money. I needed a seasonal job that left me free for the tournament circuit in the fall and the winter. I needed first-class lanes and a level of competition that would force me to throw at my best. Bingo," she said. "Rural Nova Scotia. It's all here."

"But Rollie and Catherine?" This woman, even a bowling widow, could still be a killer. "Are you just mad at them because you have to pay tax on your rental?"

Gail snorted. "That didn't help." She stopped as if struggling to get her next words out. "Name Kathy Rankin mean anything to you?"

"Which one?" I asked. We were a big family. "The one in Sydney or the one in New Glasgow?"

"Neither." Gail's face was grim. "This one lives in New Brunswick. In Moncton. She's the current top-seated ladies' pro. She won the world's last year. I want to take her out." She stared at me hard. "I shouldn't let it get to me, but when you compete at the level I do, it's how you have to be. I hyper-focus. I hear that last name, and I lose all objectivity."

I thought this over. My Scottish ancestors had understood feuds. Over the centuries, small offenses had led to long resentments. Illogical behavior was not a foreign concept to me.

"Okay, as far as I know, we're not related to a Moncton Kathy Rankin, if that's any help," I'd fixed that, but I still wanted to be sure about the rest. "But just to be clear: You didn't mess with any kitchen appliances, did you? And you didn't kill any event organizers, not even by mistake?"

"Negative," Gail said. "I did not. But that doesn't mean I don't have a good idea who did."

CHAPTER EIGHTEEN

Gail put the weight down on the table. I picked it up. I liked the color. The covering was soft, the iron inside heavy. I gripped it. The barbell felt reassuring and solid.

"You figured this out?" I asked Gail. She was full of surprises. "Who?"

"It's been a big thing in this community. I started thinking, and this is what I decided." The manager paused. "I bowl with a few of the paramedics. I've heard some things."

"Like what?"

"How it happened. That got me thinking. It could be a man because that's how men think. If they were going to kill a woman, they'd ask themselves, where would a woman go? The kitchen." She reached out and stroked the shirt again. "Not every man is like Jimbo. Not all men can see a girl's real potential."

I gave Gail a minute to herself and her memories.

"But what man?" I asked. "Maybe someone who knew Rebecca made her own coffee? But couldn't the killer also be a woman?"

"Yes. And I'm leaning that way," Gail said. "There is something subtle about this situation. It reminds me of candlepin, why women are so good at it."

"You lost me," I said. This was true.

"Look ten-pin, nine-pin, I'm sure you've seen the big heavy balls with the three holes, sixteen pounds or so. That's what you need for a game that's like, well, heavyweight boxing. In candlepin, on the other hand, our balls are around two and a half pounds. It's more a game of skill. As a sport, it's like fencing, the way women think." Gail leaned forward. "I've seen men fight after tournaments. They go into the parking lot and bash it out. When men get mad, they get violent. Women, on the other hand, are more strategic, controlled. They'll wait and get you back in the next string. Finish you off then." She leaned back, confident with her analysis. "What happened with the dishwasher was clever, neat. Anyone could do it with a screwdriver and a kitchen knife. They wouldn't need experience with semicommercial appliances, or a lot of time, only an idea."

I sat still for a moment in an empty office with a woman who I now knew was neither a murderer nor a person who made much sense. I wondered if being excellent at one thing by default made you less able at everything else. We both had our professional skills, but we were both, it appeared, amateurs at this.

"So, you're telling me that after having bowled with paramedics, you are pretty sure Rebecca Coates was killed by ..."

"The fiancée," Gail looked pleased with herself. "Had to be."

"Laura Sanders?" I thought of the woman in black linen who had bought gray baby clothes but come alive in the workshops. Was she capable of planning a murder? "How do you figure? What does she have against Rollie and Catherine?"

"Rollie? Catherine? That's not who's dead." Gail spoke slowly, as if I had missed an obvious point. "I was there when the fiancée checked in at the Inn."

Right. Gail had been there, taking the extension cords, the reason I'd figured she'd been up to no good.

"What happened?" I asked. "What was suspicious about that?"

Gail rolled her eyes. I was not catching on fast enough.

"She showed up out of the blue. Some big surprise. It was classic. Fiancé and younger tizzed-up assistant spending a weekend off in the country, where no one knows them. Woman the guy's supposed to marry drops in and catches them. Nobody's happy. I've seen it before."

"But Laura came here for my workshops," I protested. "You saw how she enjoyed herself. That's not fake."

Gail stared at me. "Please. That woman doesn't need to be taught anything. She showed me her table runner, that thing with the boats. No offense, but did you look at that stitching? Way better than the one you brought in. She didn't come here to quilt. She came to kill."

I was a little offended by the comment about my stitching. True, I'd done it by machine, not by hand, but I had used a walking foot. "But the dishwasher." I wasn't giving up. "How would she know how to do something like that?"

"Don't you know she used to work at her dad's TV station before Wallace took over?" A vague memory stirred in my mind, and I nodded. "I've been in those studios, for interviews. Cords all over the floor. They tape them down."

"She had a reason, she had a way, and she was there," I said, considering the possibilities. I'd spent three days in close contact with Laura Sanders. A murderer. And Rollie and Catherine had her sleeping upstairs. "What do we do now?"

"We have a chat with the RCMP." Gail the manager was back. "You know anyone there we can talk to?"

The officer at the front desk of the Drummond detachment recognized me.

"Come in to pay a speeding ticket?" she snickered. We both knew I'd been stopped twice for driving too slow on a 100-series highway.

I let it pass. Gail and I were there on official business. "Is Officer Nolan in?" I asked. I looked at Gail, then continued. "My friend here has something to tell the officer. Relevant to her investigation." I was pleased with myself for making our mission sound so official.

"She's not here," the officer said to me, then looked at Gail, a member of the public who impressed her more. "Up near the Inn. Someone's gone missing."

My throat went tight.

"Missing person? Who?" I croaked.

The officer behind the plexiglass stared at us. "The lady from Ontario, the one who drives the big black car, staying up there. You know the one."

"Laura. You mean Laura Sanders ?" Gail said. She and I exchanged a look.

"That's her," the officer said. "Rollie called it in. Mr. Wallace is out golfing somewhere, and Miss Sanders got fed up waiting for him, so she went for a walk. She told Rollie she was off to 'contemplate miracles,' if you can figure that one out. Anyway, when she didn't come back, it started to get dark, and her car was still there, so Catherine called here to see if she'd been seen or lost anywhere." The officer looked at me archly. "Given recent events, I think Catherine is being particularly careful about her guests."

"Did they find her?" Gail asked. "Any word yet?"

"I'm sure she'll turn up," I offered.

"You can only hope," the officer said, with little hope in her voice. "But you know how it is on that side of the island. Steep drops, rocks, water." She paused to give me a knowing look, one local girl to another. "Tourists."

CHAPTER NINETEEN

Gail and I discussed possible scenarios on our drive out to the Inn early the next morning. When we'd left the detachment the night before, we had agreed that if no news came in overnight, the best thing for us to do was to go out and see what was going on for ourselves.

We had our theories on Laura's whereabouts.

"She's taken a runner," Gail said. "It's what I would do if I was her."

I took the turn onto Shore Road. We would be there soon. "What do you mean?"

"Listen, who wants to go to jail? Nobody, right?" Gail looked out the car window as if planning her own escape. "I mean, you and I got this all figured out. It's a matter of time until the RCMP do, too." Gail crossed her arms with authority. "She's taken off before she gets caught."

"Laura said she was just going for a walk," I reminded Gail. "Maybe that's all she's done." Now that we were ready to formally deliver our suspicions, I was having my doubts. Could any woman who liked to make things as much as

Laura did be equally capable of destruction? It didn't make sense to me.

"Contemplating miracles?" she asked, rolling her eyes. "A dead giveaway. Who does that?"

Dogs, I thought, and cats. I had seen it in their faces.

"Even if you're right, and Laura killed Rebecca and has run away, what good is anything we say going to do?" The closer I got to the Inn, the more I doubted our mission.

"Civic responsibility. Looking for someone who fell off a cliff is completely different than trying to find someone who is escaping arrest," Gail said, as if tracking missing persons was something she did every day. "The RCMP have to get on it before she's gone. The airports, the border. They'll have to check bank transactions, credit cards ... maybe look into previous criminal history, known associates ..."

I stared at the woman in the seat beside me. "You seem to know a lot about police procedure," I observed.

"Not really," Gail said. "Tournaments. On the road, you spend a lot of time in motel rooms. Pay-per-view. Crime shows. Where would you go?"

"Excuse me?"

"If you were on the lam, where would you go?" The way Gail looked at me, I could tell she was interested in my answer.

This was a problem I had not given much thought to. "South America?" I said. "Isn't that where everyone goes to hide?"

"Too obvious," Gail said. "First place anyone would think of, so first place they would look. You'd think it's got to be getting crowded with criminals at this point." She looked out the car window and laughed. "Too bad for old Laura, but she left the one spot I'd go to."

"Where?" I asked.

"Right here. I don't know, people in this community are trusting. They believe everything you say about yourself." She looked over at me. "There's a lot of freedom in a place like that."

Rollie and Catherine were on the front porch of the Inn when we arrived, drinking tea. Beside them, with a striped Hudson's Bay blanket wrapped around her shoulders, was Laura Sanders.

"Oh, man," Gail said as we got out of my car. "What's she doing here?" I could tell Gail was disappointed to see our suspect alive, well, and present.

"Catherine, Rollie, Laura," I nodded to the three tea drinkers. "What happened?"

Laura put down her teacup. It was from the Royal Doulton set Rollie had inherited from our grandmother. Blue Willow, one of my favorites.

"I've known the tides on the ocean go in and out every single day. But so much water. I had no idea. Anyone could go anywhere and get cut off. Like I did." Laura picked up her cup, took a sip, and wiped her mouth with one of the napkins I had hemmed. "That information needs to be made public. People need to know."

"We'll make sure to tell them," Rollie said.

"And remind me to tell Parker when he's back from golf," Laura said. "Anyway, I went for a walk. Ran into Jane from the class. Had a chat with her. I passed an old ruin. What was it again, Rollie?"

"A bunker, essentially a room dug out of the cliff," my cousin explained. "They built them all along the coast during the war. Kind of lookouts. The one here had a gun platform."

"Ah, that explains it," Laura said. "Strange energy. Anyway, I waded out to a little island and sat down to write in my journal. You can't imagine how surprised I was when I went to go back and I couldn't. It was unbelievable."

"She was there all night until the tide went out again early in the morning," Catherine said, refilling Laura's cup. I noticed Laura had a pair of Catherine's knitted slippers on her feet, the ones she made for church bazaars. I knew these weren't Laura's regular style, but I also knew they would be cozy, suitable for wear after an all-nighter cut off by the ocean.

"That's awful," I said. "You must have been terrified."

Laura seemed surprised. "On the contrary. It was liberating, exhilarating, life-changing, and life-affirming. I had an epiphany." She smiled at Rollie as if he alone, as a former practicing psychologist, might understand. "Brené Brown was right. Sometimes, the universe speaks."

It was only on our way back into town that Gail spoke.

"Well, that was a bust," she said. "So much for Laura Sanders escaping from the law. No murderer returns to the scene and sits in a blanket, drinking tea. It doesn't mean she didn't do it, but I'm beginning to think she might be too flaky to have pulled something like that off."

"You mean the-epiphany-in-the-middle-of-the-night stuff?" I asked.

"Exactly that."

"We're not taking our theory to the RCMP?" I asked my partner in detection. "You sure about that?"

"Not at the moment, not without evidence." Gail looked gloomy. "Not even with a very good idea. Maybe we should just keep a low profile and let the RCMP handle this one."

"Probably smart," I agreed. We were even now. Gail and I had each come up with a suspect for Rebecca's murder, and we both had been wrong.

"Seems strange, though, that Arnold Palmer is never around," Gail mused. "If it was me who had been missing all night, Jimbo would have been out with a searchlight."

It occurred to me that if I were lost, Stuart would do the same.

Gail snapped her fingers. "In all this excitement, I almost forgot. You have to call Stuart."

"I do?" I asked. Had she been reading my mind?

"Yes. Sorry about that. He called when you were in class. He said something about music for a dance." Gail looked at me. "He's not sure what they want, so he thinks you should talk. Does that make any sense?"

"Bit of a long story," I said. "But I am afraid it does."

CHAPTER TWENTY

After I dropped off Gail at the visitor's center, I decided to drive by Stuart's house to see if he was home. I suspected that any conversation about the music at Seaview Manor had to happen face-to-face. There were no written words that could describe that situation.

Stuart and I both lived in bungalows built in the late 1950s. The similarity stopped there. Stuart's place was in Drummond; mine was across the causeway, in Gasper's Cove. His house had been completely renovated. Mine, inherited from my Aunt Dot, now married to a driving instructor in Florida, had not.

Stuart was outside working in his garden when I arrived. I had a thin line of petunias under my big window and a lawn of dandelion and grass. Stuart, on the other hand, had ripped up his lawn and installed an elaborate arrangement of flagstone walkways, beach rocks, feathery grasses, and wildflowers meant to attract bees in its place. Today, he was putting small plants into large pots near his front steps.

"Herbs," he said, even before I could ask. "I get more sun out front. Dill, cilantro. I need them for canning." He stood up and brushed the dirt off his hands. "You got my message? What's this going on at the Manor? Darlene's grandmother Bernadette phoned me. Something about a new playlist? She said you would explain."

"Right. The dance." What could I say that didn't make Darlene and me look like idiots? I went over and sat down on an Adirondack chair. There were two, under the shade of a huge maple planted when the house was built. "How's Erin?" I asked, trying to change the subject. Stuart's teenage daughter was one of the youngest members of the Crafter's Co-op. She and her friend Polly made friendship bracelets and earrings. Both sold very well.

"She's great, off at camp. Give me some time to catch up." Stuart was pretending this was a good thing, but I could see from his face that he was counting the days until she came home. "Listen, you know I have been going to Seaview Manor for a while now helping out at the dances?"

"Yes, I do. How did you get into that?" I asked.

"Kenny MacQuarrie, the building inspector, his dad lives there. I told Kenny once I used to be a DJ in college. That's how it started." Stuart smiled. "It's a lot of fun. I play the music my grandparents listened to. 'Smoke Gets in Your Eyes,' 'You Send Me' ... that's one of my favorites by the way."

And one of mine, too, I wanted to say, but didn't.

"So, Bernadette called you?" I asked, afraid to hear what she'd said.

"Yeah, right." Stuart dusted some peat moss off his pant legs. "Weird. She asked if for the next dance I would bring 'sock hop' music."

"Sock hop?" I tried to image what would cocnstitute sock hop music to Bernadette.

"I know. I'm thinking support stockings, not socks." The corners of Stuart's eyes crinkled. "Bernadette said you'd know what she meant."

I looked down at the watering can on the ground beside my chair. It was brass, with a long, elegant spout like a crane. The one I had at home was green plastic, with a big crack in it because I'd left it out all winter in the snow.

"She means songs that they would have played at dances when we were in high school," I said. I didn't want to betray Darlene, but I was in a corner. "Bear with me. I know this sounds nuts." I took a breath and jumped in. "George Kosoulas and Darlene were an item when we were in school. He went away to work one summer in Montreal, and she met someone else." Was there a neater way to sum up the last twenty years of Darlene's life, I wondered? "Right person, wrong time." This was sounding more implausible the more I talked. "At least, that's what George's mother thinks."

Stuart was silent for a moment. "So, when Bernadette told me George was coming to the dance, what she was really trying to tell me is that this is a setup? That Darlene, her mother, her grandmother, and George's mother are trying to stage some sort of high school dance to revive old feelings between two old sweethearts? And I'm supposed to come up with the music that makes it all happen?"

"That's almost right," I admitted. "But you should know this was mainly Sophia's idea, and Darlene is only playing along with it to be nice to her. "

"Yeah, right," Stuart said. "Are you going to be there?"

"I am," I said. "I never miss a good sock hop."

Stuart sighed, but in a way that told me he was in. "At least now one thing makes sense."

"What's that?" I asked.

"Bernadette wanted to know where they could get a good disco ball."

I remembered the last disco ball I had seen. In an old school gym, lights low, but not so low the teacher monitors couldn't see, the boys on one side of the auditorium, the girls on the other, couples shuffling over the basketball lines painted on the wood floor. I remembered the music, too.

Lyrics drifted across my mind, over the images.

"*Everybody needs somebody. You're not the only one*," I said. Why had those words come to me now?

Stuart looked at me, puzzled. "Is that a musical suggestion?" he asked.

"No," I said. "More like a premonition."

Later that evening, Toby and I were cleaning up our respective supper dishes when my phone rang.

It was Bob.

"Can you hear me?" he asked. My knitting instructor's voice sounded scratchy and faint, but I could make out what he said.

"Yes, but just barely. Where are you?" I asked.

"In the woods. I got to talk quietly, they might still be around," Bob whispered.

"Who?"

"The thieves. I have evidence. I took pictures." I heard rustling in the background, as if Bob were walking through leaves. "It makes sense. Why they took the yarn."

"Your yarn?" I asked. "You mean for your class?"

"Yes. When I unpacked my workshop supplies, it wasn't there. Two pairs of mitts were gone, too. Missing." Bob sounded more than annoyed. He sounded worried. "It's industrial sabotage. They're after my source. This is serious. I can't talk to Dawn. She's got too much on her mind. That's why I called you."

"Me? I don't have your yarn," I said. "Or your mitts."

"I didn't think so," Bob's whisper was rushed. "But you still got those contacts in the media, don't you?"

"Contacts? You mean Noah? At the *Lighthouse Online*?"

"Yeah, him." There was more rustling. "If I send you some pictures, could you forward them to him? It's a big story. An attack on the environment and a responsible local entrepreneur. Desecration."

Bob had my attention. "What? Who?"

In the background, my phone pinged once, twice, three times.

"See for yourself," Bob said. "Got to go."

I put down my tea towel and sat on a kitchen chair. I was afraid to open the attachments, to see what Bob had seen. I closed one eye and squinted with the other to blur my shock. I tapped on my phone.

Three images opened, one after the other. I stared at them, looked at Toby for support, and looked again.

I knew what I was looking at, but I didn't know why.

Bob had sent me pictures of rocks and tree trunks. I called him back.

After four rings, he picked up.

"Where are you now?" I asked. "Can you talk?"

"I'm in the car," he said. "What do you think?"

"What I think is, you sent me the wrong pictures," I said. "These are of trees."

"And? Don't you see what's missing?" Bob was impatient.

"People?" I asked.

"No, Valerie. Look closely. The lichen, none of it around the base of the trunks where I usually find it. Look further up. Can't you see the scrape marks?" Bob asked. "Someone has been in the woods, our woods, and systematically started taking out the lichen I use for dyes. I was an idiot. This is my fault. Geez, I even drew a map for them."

"A map?"

"Don't you remember? The petition. You signed it," Bob said. "It had a map on it where I found the lichen. I used a rare species for my dyes to make a political point—that's why I only used what was on the ground, not still growing. But what I have done is betray it. The lichen."

I slumped in my chair and looked at the clock on the kitchen wall. I was tired, very tired. A woman had been killed, another one trapped out on the water, and in the middle of all that, Big Bob Willet was worried about lichen. No wonder this man had never had a real job. No surprise that he was still living with his brother and his wife and didn't have a family of his own.

"Maybe you've just misplaced your yarn and the mitts," I said carefully, trying to gather what little patience I had left. "Maybe what you saw in the woods was just animals. We all need some rest. It's been a busy week."

"It wasn't animals." Bob sounded offended. "I know the difference between tools and teeth. Those pictures. Will you send them to your reporter friend and tell him I want to talk?"

I gave up. I tapped my screen. "Done," I said. "They've been sent."

"Great," Bob said. "I have so much to say."

I hoped Noah would forgive me.

CHAPTER TWENTY-ONE

It didn't take long for me to find out if he did.

It was Friday morning. I was down at the Foodmart when I ran into Noah in the baking aisle.

"Did Bob Willett reach you?" I asked cautiously.

"He did. There may be a story there, may not. We're going into the woods over the weekend to check it out," Noah shrugged. "He's a nice guy, so why not?" He paused and pointed to the four bags of sugar and stacks of mason lids in my cart and laughed. "Someone's making jam," he said.

"Yes, I am," I said. "Blueberry. I make it for the kids and send it to them. A little bit of Nova Scotia." I nodded to the jar of quick-rising yeast in Noah's hand. "Bread?" I asked.

"Nah, too much work," he said. "Pizza. Going to have some friends over to celebrate. Looks like I'll have time to cook."

"What do you mean?" I knew that Noah covered a lot of sporting events and wasn't free most weekends.

"I got East-Wested," he said. "Amalgamated out. Didn't even get a call. Just an email." He pulled out his phone from the pocket of his baggy khaki shorts and read to me. "*Due to current restructuring priorities, editorial content will now be delivered according to a new model, reducing the necessity and capacity for the local sourcing of content.*" He put his phone away and sighed. "Don't spin a spinner. I've been fired."

I was shocked. Noah was a good reporter, everyone knew that. Local people up and down the shore relied on his stories in the *Lighthouse Online* for the truth of what was happening and, more importantly, the why.

"I don't understand," I said. "How can that be?" I noticed a small tear in the ribbing at the neckline of his *East Coast Living* T-shirt. It wouldn't take me a minute to fix it. I almost offered but then reminded myself, Valerie, not everyone is your child.

"It's happening everywhere," Noah said. "Look at the local drugstores, places like this." He waved his hands across the aisle. "The Foodmart used to be Bailey's Grocery, remember?"

"I do." It was one reason local people were quick to thank us for keeping Rankin's General in the family. Independent businesses were becoming rarer and rarer every day. "I also remember when the *Lighthouse* used to be a real newspaper, before it went online." I was figuring this out. "So, this is the next step? You're going to freelance, now you've lost your job?"

"You got it," Noah said. "Investigative reporting, on my own. Those meetings at the Inn? Wallace didn't come down to welcome us into the company, he was here to check us out. Decide how many positions he could cut and still make it look like we were a genuine news outlet, which we wouldn't be. No real newsman would have acted like he did that day."

I loaded another bag of sugar into my cart. I might have time to wash the berries before I went out for the evening. "What do you mean?" I asked.

Noah looked surprised. "Think about it. We were there in the conference room the day Rebecca Coates died. A whole roomful of news people. It was chaos. There was a crime, there was the RCMP. And yet this guy, who is supposed to be the head of some kind of media empire, didn't assign any of us to the story, didn't want anyone to go check out the story. We were sent home and told to stand down. It was insane." Noah ran his hands through his hair in disbelief and remembered frustration.

"Maybe he was in shock?" I suggested. I remembered the tray Laura had carried up to the room the next day for Parker Wallace, too upset to come down. Was he upset? Or guilty?

"You don't understand," Noah said. "In the news world, nothing matters but the story, nothing. It's in our blood, but it's not in his. Outfits like East-West are just a front. News outlets are commodities to them, just vehicles to sell ads for their other interests. I checked it out. Wallace is into anything that makes him money. Real estate, hair products, fast food ..."

I knew that Noah was trying hard to sound aware, even cynical, but to me, his face looked young and hurt.

"If you go freelance, will you stay here?" I asked. Selfishly I thought, please don't move away. He surfed with my son Paul. The waves helped me keep in touch with them both.

"That's what the party's about tonight," Noah said, raising the jar of yeast. "The launch of my career as an independent writer." He had his confidence back, or was trying to make it look like he had. "Hey, why don't you come over? Bob will be there, you can talk lichen."

"I'd love to," I said, and I meant it. "But I have a dance to go to. Maybe another time. I'll bring you some jam." I hesitated, then patted Noah's shoulder as I started to wheel away. "You're going to be fine. Remember, in every crisis, there is an opportunity," I added, quoting Darlene.

Noah shrugged. I wanted him to believe me.

As I pushed my cart through the Foodmart lot, I read the license plates on the cars. It was a summertime game we played in Gasper's Cove. It was fun to keep track of who came to see us and from how far they had come. Every year, there were more and more cars, from locations farther and farther away. We all had our favorite plates; mine was Tennessee's older plates. I loved the flow of the cursive used to spell out the state's name, so artistic, a remnant of a skill regretfully no longer taught in most schools.

Ontario, Ontario, Quebec, Utah (that was a new one), Massachusetts, Vermont, Maine.

Maine? I looked closer and saw a familiar figure in the front seat, with her hand held up to her face. It was Jane, from the workshops. I was surprised she was still here. With difficulty, I pivoted the uncooperative wheels of my cart toward her car and waved when she looked up.

Jane rolled the window down, squinting in the sun. She had a plastic folder on her lap, one like a clipboard with a cover. I caught sight of a logo, a shield, and a heart. It looked familiar, but I couldn't place it.

"Still here?" I asked her. "Seeing the sights?" I noticed that the red-rimmed reading glasses she had worn to class had been replaced by large square sunglasses that were now pushed to the top of her head. Her left hand rested on the steering wheel of her car, as if she was ready to drive away. On it was the large, black, flat surface of an Apple Watch. I hadn't seen it on her before. I realized that she had been on a call when I first saw her in the car.

She answered my question with a compliment. "Great workshops," she said. "I enjoyed myself a lot. It must be a bit of a relief for you, though, to have it done." She eyed my grocery bags. "Getting life back to normal?" she asked, putting her car key in the ignition.

I have never been one for short conversations.

"I enjoyed it," I said. "I always worry, but once classes get going, I start looking forward to the next one. You must know what that's like. You must enjoy your summer break, but by the end of it, I bet you'll be ready to go back."

"Back?" Jane asked. She seemed to be keeping her eyes deliberately blank, but I sensed an increase in activity behind them.

"Yes, school," I said. "I meant to ask, what grade do you teach?"

"Grade?" she echoed, distracted. She turned the key and shifted her car into reverse. "Any of them," she replied, reaching over with her big watch hand to press a button inside the door handle. On command, the window rose up, ending the conversation and cutting me off. Behind the glass, Jane smiled, backed up, and drove away.

I stepped back and watched her go. I didn't understand what had just happened. The Jane in Bob's class had been much friendlier. What was different now? And what kind of teacher wouldn't know what grade she taught?

I moved forward and then banged my cart into a post. I got it. A Foodmart parking-lot brainwave. Only one kind of person would be unable to name the grade they taught.

Someone who was not a teacher.

This woman could knit, weave, and sew. But what else did she do?

CHAPTER TWENTY-TWO

Darlene wasn't interested in anything I had to say. She didn't want to hear about Noah's sudden lack of employment, Gail's suspicious behavior at the Foodmart, or Big Bob's disappearing lichen.

"I swear, Val, sometimes you've got a mind like a squirrel cage. Can you concentrate for one moment on what's important?" she asked. "Is this too much lip liner? Yes, or no?"

I squinted into the mirror. We were in the ladies' washroom near the front entry of Seaview Manor. Darlene hadn't wanted to make her grand entrance without a quick check of the details. My sense of déjà vu was incredible. Had Darlene and I ever left high school? It didn't feel like it.

"Is it supposed to be in two points like that on your upper lip?" I asked diplomatically. "Maybe tone it down a bit?"

Darlene leaned closer and inspected her reflection. She pulled up her lower lip and pressed it into her lipstick, then stepped back. "How's that? Better? I don't want to look like I'm trying too hard," she said.

"Then, why are you?" I asked.

"What do you mean?" Darlene snapped her evening bag closed. I looked at her outfit: a form-fitting sheath, a pair of high heels lifting her arches, and twin underwires doing the same to her breasts. She looked more like a woman on her way to the Vegas Strip than one about to enter the main dining room of a seniors' residence in Gasper's Cove, Nova Scotia.

"Why are you trying so hard?" I repeated. "I thought you told me we were only here because you didn't want to hurt Sophia's feelings. Don't tell me you have intentions of hitting on George Kosoulas tonight."

"Oh, please," Darlene said, hoisting up one of her bra straps. "If I'm going to do this, I'm going to do it right. My grandmother's here. I want to look nice."

Inwardly, I rolled my eyes. Darlene's side of the family were notorious overdressers, more the result of an attitude to life than a feel for fashion. I expected when I saw Bernadette that she'd be sporting sequins and a fresh blue rinse.

"Well, you do look good. Not so sure about myself." I looked in the mirror at the red dress and chandelier earrings my cousin had insisted I wear. "I'm up for drinking tea, but are we honestly expected to tango?"

Darlene stopped applying another layer of mascara to her lashes and looked at me. "What's the problem? Slow, slow, quick, quick, slow. That's all you have to remember." She snapped the wand of her mascara back into a bright pink cylinder. "Besides, it's only the opening number. After that, they switch to other music, more walker-friendly."

As if on cue, the strains of "La cumparista" drifted in from the hallway outside. Darlene stopped and lifted her nose, like a bird dog catching a scent.

"Show time," she said. She pulled her skirt down firmly over her hips and slammed the heavy washroom door open.

Sighing, I followed her, like I always did and always would, now in the direction of the music coming from the ballroom, once the dining room, of Seaview Manor.

I was almost there when a framed photograph caught my eye. I recognized the face. I read the brass inscription on the bottom of the frame "Pastor W. Jäger, a friend of Seaview Manor."

I was so absorbed, I didn't hear the steps behind me.

"Lovely man," a voice said. I turned to face Darlene's mother, Colleen.

"I didn't expect to see you here," I said.

"Wouldn't miss it for the world," Colleen said. She grinned, and that worried me. "I like to see my mom, and I knew you and Darlene would be here. And George. And Stuart." Colleen tried to wink, but her top lashes stuck to the bottom on that eye. Undeterred, she pried them apart, blinked a few times, and kept going. She pointed to the photo on the wall.

"Do you remember him?" she asked.

"A bit, from when I was a kid, but not well," I said.

"More's the pity," Colleen said. "He was a good man, one who left the community better than he found it. The whole family's like that—Dawn Nolan, too, in her own way. Must be the name, Jäger. It means 'hunter,' according to my grandson."

"It's nice to know the pastor made up for it," I said. "What he did before."

Colleen looked at me, her eyes making an assessment. "You mean the boats?"

I nodded.

"I have a story to tell you about that," she said. "When I was a kid, my dad used to do carpentry work at the summer camp. Whatever they needed done. Anyway, one day I was with him, and there was a fat fire in the kitchen. Very dangerous with all those kids around. Pastor Jäger ran straight into the flames, running down low, all crouched up, and put it out." She shook her head at the memory. "It was a big risk, but he didn't think about himself. My dad didn't say much, but I saw how he looked at the pastor. My father was in the merchant marine, and he said to me, 'That man's been in submarines.' I wanted to ask him what he meant, but all my dad would say was that it didn't matter anymore, and not talk about it."

"So, in a crisis, he was back in the U-boat in his mind, moving in tight spaces?" I asked.

"That's it exactly," Colleen said. "Some things you do get right into you."

Before Colleen could say anything more, Darlene interrupted us.

"Mom," she called out from a doorway across the hall. "Nana and the girls in here are asking for you. Party's just getting started."

Obediently, Colleen and I walked over and stepped across the threshold into a different world.

Darlene wasn't lying.

The Manor's former dining room was transformed. The lights had been lowered, but not too low for vision and safety reasons, and the disco ball was up, surrounded by rows of streamers and balloons. I saw Stuart near the front of the room in a vest, the kind folk singers wear, manning an old turntable, surrounded by piles of LPs. The regular rhythm of a tango vibrated out of speakers set up on tall stands, and this sound mingled with the chatter of the senior residents, family, and friends. The ladies, Darlene's grandmother Bernadette included, were arranged around tables, a full display of clip-on rhinestone earrings, ruched floral polyester dresses, strings of pearls (some costume, some inherited), and lace jackets. Two of the ladies, despite the summer weather, had glassy-eyed minks around their shoulders, taxidermic teeth clasping the copper fur. All the older ladies wore stockings. And some, those with prim faces, I suspected were also wearing worn girdles, retrieved from scented drawers where they rested between special occasions like this one.

The women at this gathering, not surprisingly, outnumbered the men. But the gentlemen were as well dressed as the ladies. All of them wore shirts and ties and some even suits, presumably saved from more business-like pasts. One of these men was talking to George, dapper himself in a sports coat over an open shirt.

Darlene and I looked at each other and split up.

Darlene zigzagged in George's direction, stopping to talk to many of the residents on her way. That left me to meander over to Stuart.

"Nice music," I said, pointing to the records. "See you've gone old school."

"Best sound," Stuart said. "Believe me. No better way to spin the classics."

"Looks like you're having fun," I said.

"How could I not?" Stuart asked. "I always feel at the end of one of these evenings that I go home with my head on straight again. I spend all my days at work with developers or municipal officials, overworked, stressed out, worn thin from trying to get ahead. Then, I go home, and I look at Erin. I second- guess everything I am doing as the parent of a teenager. It's hard to hold all those pieces together. But look at them here. The memory of the community. A whole room full of people who know exactly who they are. They have context." Stuart dropped another record. The strains of "I Only Have Eyes for You" floated across the room.

Stuart nodded at Darlene and George seated at a small table, candlelit despite the lights in the room, with a handcrafted "Reserved" sign on it, the only such sign in the room.

"Colleen will be happy George took her advice," Stuart said.

"Advice?" I asked him.

"Yes. A few days ago, Colleen went and saw George. She told him she was concerned that Darlene was a success, being deputy mayor and everything, but that she was still single. I believe her exact words were something to the effect of 'I don't want to die knowing my girl is alone.'"

I looked up at the streamers. "Is that all she said?"

Stuart gave me a sideways glance. "It gets better, but if I tell, you don't tell Darlene? Promise."

I smiled as if in agreement, but nothing said out loud, nothing in writing.

Stuart leaned in closer. I loved the way he smelled, some kind of combination of soap, good cooking, and patience. He looked around as if afraid someone would eavesdrop. "She claims that every man Darlene has married or dated since high school looks like George."

Stuart and I started to giggle like kids.

"The table for two was Colleen's idea," he said, catching his breath.

"Mothers," I laughed, including myself. "Nova Scotian or Greek, it doesn't matter. We never retire, never stop interfering."

Stuart looked past me. "Stop it," he whispered. "Here comes George."

Given the planning that had gone into the evening and the extremely romantic environment, I expected George to be happy or at least amused. Instead, he looked indignant, annoyed, and maybe worried.

"Hey, man, what's up?" Stuart asked.

"I just got a call from the hospital," George said. "Sammy Judd. He wants me to help him. It's his food truck. It's gone. A buddy called him: It's not parked where it's supposed to be. 'Judd the Spud' is Sammy's whole life. That truck is everything to him. And that guy, Kurt, who's supposed to be taking care of it? Sammy can't reach him. He's disappeared, too."

CHAPTER TWENTY-THREE

The next morning, Toby and I were in Darlene's kitchen. She and George had left the dance together in a hurry. I wanted the details.

"Sorry I took off on you like that last night," Darlene said, putting the cat bowls on the counter where Toby couldn't reach them. "Sammy wanted George to drive around and look for his food truck. I went to help him." She saw the skeptical look on my face. "In case the truck broke down somewhere. It was getting dark ... I thought maybe he might need someone to hold a flashlight."

"Right. Of course. You were dressed for roadside assistance." I poured myself a tea from the pot on the stove. "Did you find it?"

"No, but looking for it gave us time to talk." Darlene went to the fridge for milk and turned her back to me. If she thought I hadn't caught her smile, she was wrong.

"What about that Kurt Gordon guy?" I asked. "Did you find him?"

"Nope. No sign of him either," Darlene said. "What about you? How did the rest of the dance go?"

"It was fine," I said. "They packed it in early—eight o'clock is like midnight to those folks. But they had a good time. I was glad I went." I hesitated. I wanted to know more about George and Darlene but knew I wouldn't get any information from my cousin unless I offered some. "I stayed and helped Stuart pack up. Then, we went to his house. We watched a movie. It was nice." Toby looked up at me. His big dark eyes seemed to ask, *Why are we here? Our walk is supposed to be outside.* He was right. This was taking too long.

"Where did you and George end up?" I persisted.

"The look-off." Darlene opened the fridge again and examined the butter on the shelf inside the door.

The look-off? I now knew all I needed to know. It might have taken them two decades to get there, but George and Darlene were on again.

"So, what's next?" I asked.

"I think we are having lunch," Darlene said. "They're discharging Sammy this morning. George wants to go over and see him. He's going to suggest that once the truck turns up, Sammy finds someone else to take over. According to George, Kurt's not such a great cook. And there was some stuff he said he saw in Sammy's truck. Something's not right."

"What stuff?" I asked. "Not right in what way?"

Darlene came over to the table and sat down. She seemed eager to talk about something other than her love life.

"Okay, this is the deal." She put a cat on her lap. "One day, when they were both at the visitor's center, Kurt had trouble with the fryer. I guess it's old, and there's some trick to get it started. George went in to help him. When he was doing that, he noticed a bag sort of hidden behind the sacks of potatoes. Kurt went outside to check the propane line, and George had a look. He said the bag was full of fancy cameras and those long lenses. Weird, eh?" Darlene said. "Most people these days, if they want to take pictures, use their phones."

I knew the lens she was talking about. I'd seen tourists with them. They were used for long-distance, zoom-in shots.

"Maybe Kurt's a bird-watcher," I suggested.

"Does that guy look like a bird-watcher to you?" Darlene asked.

I thought of the fish-and-chip man's ponytail, his tattoos, and his poor manners. The one thing I knew about bird-watchers was that they were polite.

"No, he doesn't," I admitted. He looked more like a criminal. I wondered if he was.

After Toby and I left Darlene's, we went for a long walk. I felt that Toby deserved it for his patience and self-restraint during a visit to a house full of cats. And I needed time to think. What Darlene had said scared me. What if Kurt wasn't who he said he was? He certainly wasn't suited for selling fish-and-chips, but what if that was a front for the real reason he was here? Why was he taking long-range pictures? Where was he now? Did he have anything to do with Rebecca's death? Had he tried to kill Rollie once, and would he try again? My intuition told me that bad things weren't over, they were just getting started.

I grabbed my phone and, fingers fumbling, called my cousin.

“Bluenose Inn,” Rollie answered. I thought I detected a wariness in his voice. “How can I help you?”

“Rollie! You’re still there,” I said. “How’s Catherine?”

“We’re both here—we could be better, but we’re here,” he answered.

Something was wrong. I knew it.

“What’s happened?” I asked, tightening my grip on Toby’s leash to turn him around. I had to talk to the RCMP. Get out to the Inn myself. Warn everyone that Kurt might be coming for them before it was too late.

“Reservations,” Rollie said. “We’ve been taking calls all morning. Cancellations. The story’s out. An unsolved murder at a Nova Scotia bed-and-breakfast. No one wants to come here if they think there’s still a killer on the loose. They’re too afraid.” I could hear Catherine’s voice in the background, her voice urgent as she tried to join the conversation. “I can’t say I blame them.”

“Rollie, look, this is important. Put me on speaker. You both need to hear this.” I waited until I heard Catherine’s voice before I continued. “I have a feeling I know what happened to Rebecca. And I don’t want to scare you, but I think that guy who has been driving around in the ‘Judd the Spud’ truck is not who he says. He’s probably not even using his real name. I think he’s someone from your past in the prison, Rollie, somebody with a grudge against you. I’ve got Duck checking it out. I want you and Catherine to lock up and stay put while I call the RCMP. You got that?”

“Not necessary.”

I heard a new voice on my phone, gravelly, familiar, and amused.

"Officer Nolan's already here. Why don't you come out, too? Coffee's on."

My hand went tight around my phone. I dropped Toby's leash.

"Oh, and by the way," the voice said. "You got it wrong. My name really is Kurt."

CHAPTER TWENTY-FOUR

When I arrived at the Inn, I opened the car door and let Toby out to run around. Apart from an RCMP cruiser and the "Judd the Spud" truck, the parking lot was empty. Even Laura's black Lexus was gone. Business, as Rollie said, didn't look good.

I followed the sound of voices into the front room. Catherine was in one of the tartan wing chairs, Rollie behind it. Officer Nolan was perched uncomfortably on an ancient and stern Victorian settee that I knew from experience was hard, lumpy, and unforgiving.

Only Kurt, the unreliable fish-and-chip man, seemed at ease.

A tray of tea and some of Catherine's scones were on the small table in front of the group. Only Kurt had one of the bone-china cups in his hands.

"Gang's all here," I said as I walked through the double arches from the hall. When I was nervous, I had a bad tendency to revert to clichés. "Sammy's looking for his truck. Does he know you are here?" I asked Kurt.

"He does now." Kurt leaned over to slide his cup back onto its saucer next to the plate of scones. "Things were slow, so I went for a drive up the coast. I must have missed Sammy's calls." He turned to look at Rollie. "Do you know how bad cell phone reception is around here?" he asked. "I only got one bar."

"It's been mentioned," Rollie said. "Depends on who your provider is. Glad we had a landline you could use when you stopped by."

Catherine cleared her throat and looked around the room. "Speaking of calls, we all heard yours, Valerie. You have to stop worrying about us. Officer Nolan is here to tell us how her investigation is going. We thought that was important information for us to have, given all these cancellations. You might as well hear it too."

Kurt made a move as if to get up. "Maybe I should go?" he asked.

"I have nothing to say that won't be in our public statements," Nolan said. "I don't think that's necessary. The more people who have the facts, the less gossip and false speculation there will be to deal with." She looked straight at me. "As we all know, that is a common scenario in this community."

I avoided her gaze and picked up a scone. Mine were never this light. When things settled down, I had to get Catherine's recipe.

"We get it," Rollie said with uncharacteristic irritation. "The question is, how close are you to making an arrest? That poor woman needs justice. And we need to find a way to manage public fear. This ambiguity is ruining us."

Catherine reached up and laid her hand over the one Rollie had on her shoulder. "Let's be blunt," she said, always the one to do it. "We feel terrible this happened to one of our guests, of course we do. But it wasn't our fault. Until you find out who did this, nobody's going to believe that. Nobody will trust us. We need something we can tell people, and so far, you haven't given us anything."

This was the wrong thing to say to Officer Dawn Nolan. Ex-librarians and brand-new innkeepers weren't going to tell her that she wasn't doing her job.

"Our investigation is proceeding exactly as it should," she bristled. "You can have confidence in that. We are looking at the victim's life, her associations, and events leading up to her visit here. I feel we are making significant progress."

That's not telling anyone anything, I thought to myself. I looked over at the strained look on Rollie's face and decided I had something to add.

"You're not telling us if Rebecca's death was an accident or if the killer was out to get someone else." I didn't name Rollie and Catherine, but everyone in the room knew who I meant. "There's lots of possibilities. My mind is full of them. It's all I can think about."

Nolan stared at me. "If you have anything solid, by all means, share it, but I suggest you don't get carried away. We are trained to do this—you aren't."

"Then do a better job. This isn't playing with toy soldiers or model boats, this is the real thing," I blurted out, then, when I saw the stricken look on Nolan's face, regretted it. "No one in this community feels safe," I continued. "Whoever was behind this death could be someone we know, or we don't. Someone who is passing through or comes from away, who is still here or gone. It's making us do crazy things." I realized that I could be talking about myself but pushed that thought aside. "Finding bowling shirts and thinking it's evidence. Figuring a fish-and-chip truck is an escape vehicle. Thinking that bird-watchers don't have tattoos."

I paused, aware of the discomfort in the room. Rollie and Catherine fidgeted and studied the view outside the window. Nolan tightened her mouth in annoyance. Only Kurt seemed to listen to me, with a look in his eyes I was surprised to see: respect.

Nolan stood up, shaking out the creases in her pants. "I came here, Rollie and Catherine, to say we are doing everything possible as expeditiously as we can. We have divisions at many levels working on this. I have no doubt we will be able to give you something more concrete soon. Then, you will have information to share with your guests. Sound reasonable?"

"It does," Rollie said. I noticed him tighten his grip on Catherine's shoulder, holding her back from saying more. "Thank you for coming."

Kurt was on his feet. "I'll walk out with you," he said to Nolan. "I should leave. I think I'll swing into town and see Sammy." For a moment, I had a flash that there was something personal in Kurt's interest in the female RCMP officer, but shook that idea aside.

"I guess I should go, too," I said. "Toby knows to stay on the property, but I better check on him." I stopped. "You have lids on the compost bins, don't you?" I asked Rollie.

"Of course," my cousin said. "Because of the raccoons. But before you leave, I'd like a word. Let's go out the back way."

I followed Rollie out to the porch. Toby was near it, lying in the grass, a large stick in his paws, not a care in the world.

"What do you want to talk about?" I asked. There must be some new information, a detail Rollie hadn't wanted to share in front of our fish-and-chip visitor or the law.

Rollie leaned forward and put his large hands on the railing that ran between the posts of the porch. He looked out onto the ocean at the end of the property.

"You," he said. "I want to talk about you."

"Me?" I wasn't expecting this. "Why me?"

Rollie turned around. He had his I-am-the-older-cousin face on, the one that always irritated me. "Did you hear yourself in there?" he asked. "Rattling on about bowling shirts and food-truck getaways." I could tell by the expression on his face that Rollie wanted to say, "People think you are nuts," but stopped himself. Licensed psychologists don't use words like that.

We'd had this conversation before. "You want me to tone it down?" I asked.

"I have some concerns," Rollie said, in a more professional voice than I liked. "First, I want to tell you I recognize your strengths. Like so many highly creative people, you are quick, you can make connections, and you see things most of the rest of us miss."

"Thank you," I said. "I appreciate that. I think all of us in the Crafters' Co-op are the same way—that's why we all get along." I made my way over to the steps down from the porch to the grass. It was time I took Toby home.

Rollie held up a hand, like a stop sign. "I'm not finished," he said. "I also think that sometimes you see things that aren't there. Then, you build up fantasies, go from one thing to another, inventing"—he searched for the right word—"conspiracies. Accusing people of things they didn't do. You've done it before, got the wrong idea and made mistakes."

I knew what my cousin was referring to. There had been some incidents in the community in the past, and I had been in the middle of them. "But I got a lot right, too. Remember that."

"I do," Rollie admitted, "but I'm wondering if now it wouldn't be useful for you to have a chat with an old colleague of mine. A lovely man, he has experience with neurotypical disorders—not that I am saying that is your issue, but you might need some support right now, given the trauma of recent events."

I had heard enough. All I was trying to do was take care of the people I loved. Including the one talking down to me on his own back porch.

"I don't need to see anyone," I said, and because I didn't have Rollie's university education, I added, "I am not crazy, and I am going to prove it."

CHAPTER TWENTY-FIVE

I kept my phone charged and close to me the rest of the day. I expected Rollie to call me to apologize. I wanted him to say he was sorry for thinking my desire to protect him, or any other member of our family, was a mental-health issue. If there was something wrong with getting involved in each other's lives, then all of Gasper's Cove needed treatment.

A call from him never came.

In my heart, I didn't blame him. It wasn't Rollie's fault that he was overeducated or that he had forgotten that some of life's stressors were to be endured, and maybe outsmarted, before they could be dismissed. Even if he didn't call, I knew that I would eventually forgive my cousin.

I wished that I could say the same thing about myself.

I had broken a trust out there at the Inn, the first rule of hobbyists everywhere. With one casual comment, I had let down every knitter who had come late to a dinner party because she had just one more row. With a slip of the tongue, I had betrayed every admin assistant who had ever printed off a sewing pattern on the office copier after hours. With only a few words, I had violated the crafters' agreement to never let anyone from the outside know how much our secret lives meant to us.

I'd made known, in public, that RCMP Officer Dawn Nolan played with toys.

It would be a long time before she would trust me again. I wouldn't blame her.

The person who had to apologize was me.

The plexiglass officer answered the phone.

"Oh, you," she said. "Officer Nolan is out. Can I take a message?"

"No, thanks, it's a personal matter," I explained.

"Then, why call here? That sounds like an after-hours issue. Why don't you just wait and tell her when you see her next? Or write her a letter. Send her a note." The woman, who spent her days surrounded by plastic, chuckled at her wit. I didn't know that you could hear a smirk.

"Okay, then," I said, attempting to sound more reasonable than I felt. "Tell her I called. And thank you so much for your help."

I hung up and considered my options. A written apology was not such a bad idea. I had the right card, one of the many we sold at the Co-op, a watercolor piping plover dancing across the sand. It hit the right note, I decided, between personal and respectful, which was exactly what I needed. I found a pen that still wrote. I composed a short message.

Sorry if I was unprofessional, you never are. Won't happen again. I hesitated, then continued. *Good luck finding the killer.*

I couldn't help myself. *If you need assistance, let me know. Best regards, Valerie.*

That done, I decided to hand-deliver the card. Even if Dawn Nolan wasn't home, I would still drop in and see Sylvie. Her wreath workshop had been one of the week's highlights. I wanted to thank her for doing it.

When I arrived at Sylvie's house, she was on her hands and knees alongside Big Bob, picking dandelions from her lawn. I put my card in the mailbox marked 124b and went to talk to them.

"Good gardeners," I said. "I should go home and do the same at my house."

Bob's head snapped up. "If you do, save the flowers for us," he said. "Sylvie and I have a new project. Dandelion dye. We're thinking of forming a partnership. Weeds are the way to go. Easier to access, large, widely available quantities. They are much more suited for the mass market than lichen. We'll save that for our premium line."

"You should see the dye we can make," Sylvie added. "The more blossoms, the more intense the yellow. And it's permanent, like turmeric, but less expensive, and there's no need to import supplies. It's the ultimate grow-local product. Like henna."

"Henna?" I asked. "What does that have to do with anything?"

"A shrub," Sylvie answered. "Used all over the world and it comes from a shrub." She touched her hair, which I noticed had a golden glaze to it. I looked at Bob. His beard had the same yellowish tint. They looked like pictures in an old newspaper.

"Dandelions are more sustainable than commercial dyes," Bob said. "That's why we are under such pressure to get a process we can patent. It's a real rush-to-market situation. As soon as the big corporations realize how much cheaper it is to work with natural sources, they'll be all over it, once they finish with the algae." He paused from his harvest and surveyed the street for listening ears. "I'm no fool. I have evidence that the big capital investors are already here."

"Who?" I asked. Sylvie kept digging. I suspected that she'd heard this story before.

"That Parker Wallace character. News is a minor part of his business. I looked into it. He's got a hand in everything, heavily into food and the personal-care sector." Bob looked around again and lowered his voice to a whisper.

"And the man's a liar. He's covering the real reason he's here," Bob said. "I think he's checking out land to buy to set up a commercial algae operation, the fast food of the future. I've got Larry tracking him with the blimp. He told me he was watching things for you, and that gave me the idea. Anyway, guess what? This Wallace claims he's going around the province because he has meetings with news outlets. But that's not what he's up to."

"What's he doing then?" I asked. I knew that Laura believed in the meetings. It was how she explained her fiancé's absences.

Sylvie stood up and rubbed the yellow stains on her hands. "Golfing. My husband was up in Inverness and saw him at Cabot Links."

"Do you know how expensive it is to golf there?" Bob asked. I shook my head. I had no idea. "Lots—believe me, lots. The only people who go there to golf are those with money or those trying to impress money. It's also where you go when you want to have a private business conversation. Like with investors."

"That's right," Sylvia said. "Apparently, Wallace is there a lot. My husband saw him in a foursome just this week. With someone else we know well. *Really* well."

"Who was that?" I asked.

"That friend of yours," she said. "That engineer. Stuart Campbell."

CHAPTER TWENTY-SIX

I stood on Stuart's front steps and rang the bell.

The door opened.

It was Stuart's daughter, Erin.

"You're back," I said. "How was camp?"

"Awesome," Erin said. "Polly and I were in the same cabin. If we didn't want to swim, they let us do crafts."

That sounded like my kind of camp.

"You'll have to show me what you made," I said. "Bring it in next time you're at the Co-op."

"I will, definitely." Erin appraised me. "Are you here to see my dad?"

"I am," I said. "Is he in?"

"No, not right now. It's bowling night, he won't be back until after eight. Why don't you go over and watch him?" she asked, her face composed, her blue eyes, the same as her father's, animated. "He'd like that."

I doubted there was a small town in Canada that didn't have a version of Starlite Lanes. These local bowling alleys were always situated on the road in or out of town and in rural communities were often the only place to go for entertainment that could not be met by the Legion, the church, or the Odd Fellows Hall. Most of these establishments had been built in the 1950s and had stayed there in time. They had jitterbug names, like Thunder Bowl, the Esquire, AlleyCats, and Bowl-a-Rama. As I passed the Starlite, I saw Stuart's car in the lot. Remembering his daughter's smile, I decided to go in and see him.

Inside, the Starlite was exactly the way I'd left it as a teenager decades ago. There was the same clatter of balls hitting hardwood. The same clang of the candlepins as they ricocheted across the end of the lanes, since according to the rules of this game, they could not be reset between throws. I could smell the familiar scent of deep-frying in the air. I took note of the rows of flat, long-laced shoes, still in their cubbies behind the desk, divided by size.

I could tell right away that it was League Night. Off to the right, I saw Gail with a group of serious men. Closer to me, in a center lane, I saw Stuart and Kenny, the building inspector, playing against a fisherman and Harry Sutherland, the yacht club manager. Stuart's group had finished their string and apparently were the losers. I waited while they shook the hands of the bowlers in the next lane and made their way to the canteen.

Stuart stopped when he saw me.

"Didn't expect to see you here."

"Didn't expect to be here," I answered. "Erin told me this was where I'd find you. I'd like to talk, if you have some time."

"Sure. Give me a minute to finish up with the guys. I'll meet you out front. Okay?" I could see the question on Stuart's face. How was I going to ask him what I'd come to say?

I went outside to the parking lot and leaned against the hood of my car. There was a strange feeling of familiarity to this, to be in this place waiting for a guy, that reminded me of high school. This made me think of George and Darlene. Was it possible to go back in time, or when a moment had passed, was it for forever?

The door of the bowling alley opened. Stuart walked out.

"Sorry, I had to congratulate Gail," he said. "She's out of my league, literally. That woman is a real pro, a killer." He looked at me and laughed. "I know how your mind works. Maybe I shouldn't say that with you around."

"Don't worry," I said, waving his words away. "I eliminated her as a suspect days ago." I decided to change the subject. "So, what got you into bowling?"

"Kenny," Stuart said. "We were talking on-site one day. I told him that now Erin's getting older, she doesn't need me at home every evening." I detected a note of regret in his voice. "I was looking for something to do. It's fun. I like it better than golf, to tell you the truth."

This surprised me. I understood why Sylvie didn't want to golf. She had rope weaving and drainpipe knitting to do. But Stuart?

"Why's that?" I asked. It seemed to me that golfing was something every responsible engineer did.

Stuart came and stood beside me, leaning on the hood like I was, waiting for a group of excited bowlers to walk by, before he answered. "For a start, golf's expensive. Being out on the course is often an excuse to talk business or to complain about your swing, your putt, handicaps, pros, and golf simulators." He paused as if just realizing something. "Golf's a lot about complaining."

"And bowling? I mean, you can't compare them. A different crowd," I said, watching the evening's league competitors drive away.

"Exactly," Stuart said, pleased I understood. "That's the thing about candlepin—anyone can do it. When I bowl with the guys, we often have a couple of seniors in the lane on one side and a family on the other. There's a dad in a wheelchair there every week with his kids. And everybody's having a good time, even the real competitors."

"So, you bowl with Kenny," I said. "Who do you golf with?" I was interested in what Bob had told me about Parker Wallace, but I also wanted to know more about Stuart's social circle. I wondered if there were any Cabot Links females in his cart.

"Usually corporate types," Stuart answered. "Those new courses they built in Cape Breton really turned those little communities around, gave them jobs they needed. Kept more young people home. You see small planes with players flying in all the time. But those courses aren't cheap. If I can play with someone in business, I can write off the greens fees as an expense. This month, I've joined up with a contractor I often work with and Parker Wallace, who is a terrible putter by the way, and Kurt, the fish-and-chip guy.

Now, that's someone who can hit a ball. But he's careful not to show Parker up."

This got my attention. "Excuse me?" I asked. "Wallace has to be worth millions. What's he doing with a guy who sells chips out of a truck window?" As soon as I said it, I remembered Kurt at the meeting at the Inn. There had been a composure and a confidence about him that had surprised me.

"I know, the odd couple, right?" Stuart said. "But we have no idea what Kurt does the rest of the year when he's not here, do we? He's vague about that. Plus, you can't judge anyone by how they look, but their clubs say a lot. Kurt's are top-of-the-line." Stuart shook his head. "All Wallace wants to talk about is golf-course development. Kurt listens, and he seems interested in the area. He knew I did the inspection on the Inn. He even knew Rollie had been a psychologist with the government. And he wanted to know how much Rollie paid for the Inn and how business was. He couldn't figure out why someone would leave a secure career to come back here. Wallace had to remind him it's the view that counts." Stuart looked at me. "You know, the north side of the island would be a great investment for anyone who wanted to develop another golf course."

"The north side of Gasper's?" I asked. "That's where the yacht club is. Where a lot of my crafters live, and Rollie and Catherine. What would happen to the Inn?"

"It would make a helluva clubhouse, wouldn't it?" Stuart said. "An old sea captain's home, right on the cliff? Can't you just see it?"

I was afraid I could. And I knew that I wasn't the only one.

CHAPTER TWENTY-SEVEN

Stuart and I stayed like that for a while, shoulders touching, leaning up against a dusty car in the parking lot of a small-town bowling alley until the intensity of the romantic venue got to be too much for us. I mumbled something about needing to catch up on things, not sure what those were, and Stuart looked at his watch, a good old-fashioned one with numbers and hands, and said that it was time he went home to Erin. Before he left, I asked Stuart how likely it was that anyone could develop the north side of the island as a golf resort. His answers, based on what had happened in other communities, were not encouraging. Anything that could bring in tourists and jobs was likely to receive provincial, municipal, and public support, he told me. If someone came in with enough money, there would be no way to stop them. He didn't say it, because he didn't have to, but a new bed-and-breakfast, doing little business, wouldn't stand a chance against a determined developer.

As I watched Stuart drive off, I felt more alone than I had in a long time. Rather than admit that I was lonely, I tried to distract myself with the content of our conversation. There was something familiar about the pieces of the puzzle I was trying to assemble. What was it?

Then, it came to me.

This process reminded me of quilting.

Trying to figure out the events of the last week had suddenly returned me to the stage when I had been making Catherine's table runner and all the pieces started to look like the final product. If this were a table runner, all that would be left to do was the binding, once I had cut it to fit.

But this wasn't quilting. It was a far more complicated and dangerous situation. No piece had been put in upside down, nothing could be unpicked and fixed. Someone had died.

I couldn't do the finishing on my own. I needed to talk this through, but with who?

I called Darlene.

It went immediately to voicemail. I left a message.

Rollie?

He was always there for me, but I was afraid if I shared my theories, he'd only see them as another reason why I needed to see his friend, the shrink.

Dawn Nolan?

Even if she would talk to me, after my toy-boat slip, what did I have to give her? That two guys played golf together? That they might be investing in local property? There was nothing to interest the RCMP there.

I needed more solid information. Something that would link Parker Wallace and food-truck Kurt with expensive clubs and a scheme large enough to cause a lot of trouble.

Who would give me that?

I had only three potential sources.

Duck, Noah, and Larry Beal, the blimp guy.

I'd asked Larry to look around. Duck had promised to access his family's criminal network. Noah was writing a book and had researched East-West Media.

I flipped my phone onto the car speaker and called the young reporter first.

"Hey, Val," he said when he answered. "What's up?"

"Lots," I answered. "Are you at home? I'd like to talk to you about Parker Wallace."

"My former-employer-for-five-minutes?" Noah sounded interested. "I'm just waxing my board. Come on over."

I'd been to Noah's place near the beach several times in the past, dropping off my New York surfer/pastry-chef son Paul when he was home for a visit. Noah lived in a house shaped like a large shed, with timber construction, a roof on an angle, and a large glass wall that faced the waves. It was a simple home but comfortable, with two small bedrooms at the back and a kitchenette with a counter and stools in the front. It was furnished with a standing desk and a leather couch draped with handwoven blankets Noah had brought back from surfing trips to Mexico, Peru, and Indonesia. I liked going there; it was a glimpse into the lives my children lived wherever they were now.

But today, I was there on a more serious mission. I had questions, and I hoped that Noah had answers. I parked my car in the rutted sand and rock behind Noah's house. I walked past two long black neoprene wetsuits, sagging on a line strung near the outdoor shower, to the front sliding door. I looked in the window. Noah was inside, pushing down the plunger of a French-press coffeemaker. I rapped on the glass. He looked up and came over to open the door.

"You caught me," he said. "My mom. She always says, 'Whenever anyone drops by, make coffee before they get there.'"

"Thank your mother the next time you see her," I laughed. "How's the book going?" I put my purse on the floor next to the couch and pulled up a stool.

"Great," he said. "I'm working on the part where the trail went cold in each case. You would think that even if they couldn't catch the crooks, more of the stuff they took would show up eventually. But that's the thing: It turns out that disposing of stolen goods is an art in itself. The paintings they took from the Museum in Montreal? There's no record of a public sale. But," Noah paused dramatically, "that doesn't mean they aren't in a private collection somewhere. They could be hanging in some summer home down the road. We'd never know. Same goes for the cash the Assiniboine Bandit took. Vanished."

I tried to remember the other cases Noah had talked about. "But what about money in, what was it, the Toonie Heist? Wouldn't that be easier to trace? It's not as if you could suddenly start paying the rent and buying groceries with nothing but two-dollar coins. People would notice."

"Ah, they wouldn't do that," Noah said, pouring me a coffee into a hand-thrown pottery cup. "There is always a middle stage—they call it "money laundering"—a place to put the cash and then live off it another way. Suppose you had a way to roll that change up and deposit it in banks across the country, in some system? That would make sense."

I had an image of Darlene and me sitting on the floor of my living room in front of the coffee table at home, rolling buckets of coins. "But that would take forever, and so much organization," I protested. "Who would do that?"

"Someone with a million and a half reasons," Noah said, offering me the milk. "That's how they usually catch these guys, by figuring out where the money went. The cops look for property that has been recently purchased, anonymous donations to private charities and organizations, or someone living larger than their means. Look what happened to Paddy Mitchell."

"Paddy Mitchell?" I asked. I was lost, but the name seemed familiar.

"He was the brains behind the Stopwatch Gang," Noah explained. "Paddy wore a stopwatch around his neck. His crew took whatever they could get in 90 seconds. It was an usher at church who did him in—the guy noticed $100 bills in the collection plate. That's the point. Getting rid of the money is the hard part."

Noah was quiet. "But you are not here to discuss my book, are you?" he asked. I noticed that he had made the switch to being the one who asked the questions. The reporter in him was back.

"No, you're right," I said. "You looked at East-West Media. I want to know if it is possible that Parker Wallace is down here, not because he bought up businesses like the *Lighthouse* but because he wants to develop a golf course. What do you think?"

Noah took a sip of his coffee before he spoke. "It's possible, I guess. It never made a lot of sense that he wanted us, to be honest," he said. "Print is dead, anyone can post news online.

The future belongs to big news organizations and local, small, community-based news. The mid-sized small-town papers, online or not, are on their way out. So, why would he be buying those now?"

"Put like that, it doesn't make sense," I admitted. Wistfully, I thought of how important the daily newspaper had been to my family growing up. Where were all those paper boys now? The ones who came by once a week to collect, the ones who found something extra every year in their Christmas cards? "But I got the impression from Laura that Parker was some kind of crack business mind, someone who had cash for anything he wanted to do. Was that not right?"

"It's part of his act," Noah said. "When I started to dig, I realized Wallace has spent most of his life bluffing, living close to the wire. There are a couple of near bankruptcies in his past. If it wasn't for Rebecca Coates, he wouldn't have lasted."

"Rebecca? The one who died? I thought she was just his PR person, someone he met when she was a young reporter."

"I guess she was that, too," Noah said. "But everyone I talked to said she was the real brains in that business, the one you had to talk to if you wanted to get anything done. An old-school admin assistant who really ran the business and made the boss think he was smart. A lot of women spent their careers doing that. I should know, my mom was one of them. And they were never paid enough for what they do," he added.

"So, are you telling me that if Wallace was about to get involved in a major development project, Rebecca would have known about it and was probably right in the middle of it?" I asked.

"Based on what I heard, I'd say absolutely," Noah said. "If Wallace was doing something big, she would have been the one making it happen. Unless"—Noah stopped and looked at me—"she didn't think it was a good idea."

CHAPTER TWENTY-EIGHT

I stared at Noah.

Was it possible that Rebecca had for some reason interfered with, or at least disagreed with, a project between Parker Wallace, not the financial wizard his fiancée thought he was, and food-truck Kurt? Could Kurt be an investor with money from sources unknown? I felt that I was on to something. If the land was important enough for someone to kill for, Rollie and Catherine could still be in danger. I had to talk to Duck and Larry. I needed more information.

I hardly noticed when Noah stood up and looked past me out to the water. When I did, I recognized the look.

"The waves?" I asked.

"Yeah, sorry," Noah said. "Is there anything else I can help you with?" He studied me. "I haven't said much, you know. This business stuff on Wallace is a matter of public record. I hope you aren't going to try and draw any conclusions from it."

"No, of course not," I said, hoping that Noah believed me. My hand was already in my pocket around my phone.

I could call Larry and then go to the store to see Duck. I reached over to the floor beside the couch and picked up my bag.

"Enjoy your surf," I said. "I've got some errands to run." I let myself out and walked quickly around the side of the house to make my call. I realized then that I didn't have Larry Beal's number. Sylvie would. I opened my car door, snapped on my seatbelt, and called her.

"Sorry to bother you," I said when she answered. "I need to talk to Larry. Do you know how I can reach him?"

"Good luck with that," she said. "When he and that blimp take off, he is unreachable. His phone is off. I think he doesn't like to waste his time talking."

"How do you contact him?" I asked.

"Sometimes he calls me, you know, to meet him beside the road, but most of the time, I go by his place. If he has rope for me, he leaves it out on the porch or with Gail."

"Gail?" I asked. "What does she have to do with rope?"

"Nothing. He rents that cottage she has."

"Okay. I'll get in touch with her."

"You could try that," Sylvie said, "but she has trouble tracking him down, too. What we both usually do is leave him a note on the door. He pays attention to those."

"Where is this cottage exactly?" I wanted to see Duck before he left for the day. I was running out of time.

"The directions are complicated, it's hard to find," Sylvie said. "Down a steep road, right on the water. You'd never find it if you didn't know it was there." She paused. "Listen. I'm due to go tomorrow, but I could go tonight. If he's there, I'll tell Larry you want to talk to him. Or I'll leave a note. That help?"

"Are you sure?" I asked. "It's not too much trouble?"

"Nope," Sylvie said. "If I leave late enough in the day, Mr. Golfer will have to make supper and feed the kids."

"Thanks. I really appreciate it."

"Don't mention it," Sylvie said. "If Dad's here, the kids will never miss me."

Darlene was leaving the store just as I arrived.

"What are you doing here?" I asked. "Shopping or seeing your mother?"

"My mom," Darleen said. Behind her, Colleen waved to me from behind the cash counter. "I need her to get my grandmother to tone down this George thing."

"Why? What's she up to?" I couldn't imagine that the long arms of Bernadette's matchmaking could reach very far from Seaview Manor.

"Trouble," Darlene said. "She has some old lady she knows in Halifax checking with the Greek Orthodox priest about the procedure for conversion. She says she's interested in general information, like suddenly at eighty-eight years old, this is something she needs to know."

"Relax. George knows what she's like. He'll think it's funny." I noticed then that Darlene had on a cross-over knit top, the one with the coral flowers that brought out the color in her hair. She also had on earrings I hadn't seen before. They matched her outfit. "You're looking all done up. Where are you going?"

Darlene tried to look vague. As if that would ever fool me.

"Down to the Agapi."

"It's Monday. They're closed," I pointed out.

"I'm going there to meditate. Sophia asked me. Between George and his father. Something about putting in a takeout window." Darlene pulled the cross-over of her top over, as if trying to make herself look more official.

"Conversion could be a good thing," I teased. "Do you know the Greeks do Easter on a different day? Next year, you could end up with two dinners."

"Oh, please," Darlene said, attempting a new tone for her, innocence. "That's not what tonight's about. Sophia is a nice lady. She thinks they'll fight less if I am around." With that, Darlene moved past me to head out the door and down the street to the Kosoulas family restaurant. I hurried out to catch her. I had an idea, and I needed hard evidence. "Wait," I called out. "I need you to ask George to do something."

Darlene turned around and crossed her arms. "What do you want?"

If I couldn't explain this to Darlene, I couldn't explain it to anyone. "Look, it's about Rebecca dying. It's a long story, but I am beginning to think that Kurt is doing a deal with Parker Wallace." I knew enough not to get into the golf idea with Darlene. That would make it sound complicated, and I wanted her to stay with me. "Remember those cameras George saw in the fish-and-chip truck?" The talk of a takeout window had reminded me. "Those big lenses, for distance? Why is Kurt, who we know nothing about, taking long-range pictures?"

Something connected with Darlene. I could see it in her face. Our town was her town, and the idea of someone spying in it got her attention. "How does George fit into this?" she asked.

"I want him to tell Officer Nolan about that camera equipment. It's just too weird that this guy is driving around in a food truck, taking pictures on the sly." I hoped that the RCMP officer would agree with me on that. "If there are photographs, she should see what they are. She's investigating a murder; she has a right to ask."

Darlene processed what I said. "You're right. It is weird. It can't hurt to tell her. I'll mention it to George. On one condition."

"Name it," I said. I needed some action; I would agree to anything.

"Go in there and tell my mother George and I are just friends. Old friends. Can you do that?"

I nodded but didn't promise anything. There was no point. Colleen and her mother had their minds made up.

As it turned out, Colleen was with a customer when I went back into the store, so I was spared having to lie to her. That was just as well. I heard the sound of heavy cardboard being ripped at the back of the building. That meant Duck was down there working. And he and I were due for a chat.

I found our handyman near the rear landing, wrapping twine around the stacks of packing boxes he had disassembled.

"Thanks for that," I said. "We can get that out for recycling Tuesday."

"Only doing my job," Duck grunted, turning away from me. He was not in a very chatty mood. I walked around to where he could see me.

"Listen," I began, "I don't want to bug you, but I'm thinking about Rollie. Were you able to find out anything from your brothers?"

Duck sighed. "It's not that easy," he said. "You don't understand. Getting information from a prison takes time." He searched for a way to make me understand. "Asking those guys about something, it's not exactly like I'm Googling it. You know what I mean?"

"I get that," I said, looking around to see if anyone could hear us. "But did you find anything out?"

"Bits and pieces. Hard to tell." Duck stopped talking, like that was all he had to say.

I had no patience for this, not today. "Talk to me. I can take it," I said. "Is someone out to get Rollie?"

"Not that I can make out," Duck said. "The word is, Rollie was one of the good guys. They miss him. Wish he was back. The new guy that took over his counseling job? Guess what he's making them do? Journaling. They hate it. Rollie used to play cards and let them talk."

"I see," I said, and I did, sort of.

"Anything else?"

Duck looked uncomfortable. "You got to know that most of this came to me through my cousin Wiggy, you know, the one who's been bald since he was a teenager?"

"I remember him. What did he say?"

"Well, Wiggy is not the most reliable person, lies like a carpet most of the time, but he can generally call a mood, if you know what I mean?"

I wasn't sure. "What mood did Wiggy pick up?" I asked as patiently as I could.

"The boys are worried. Rumor is that some big operators, we're talking out west, Toronto, maybe even Montreal, who knows, are taking an interest in this area. Some kind of an operation being set up. The local boys can't figure it out. It's got them spooked."

"Spooked?"

"Yeah, that's what Wiggy told me," Duck said. "Not good, outsiders coming in. Our guys like to see things coming, get ahead of it, and with this one, they can't. You gotta understand, what we run around here is more like what you'd call *disorganized* crime."

I had no points of reference for the world Duck was talking about. Paranoia was rare among crafters. The only thing that terrified us was missing a good sale. This was interesting, but not specific enough for me to make sense of it.

"Okay, if real criminals ..." I searched for the right word and found it. "If the *Mob* is following something going on down here, what is it?"

"That's the thing, right?" Duck picked up the lid of a cardboard box and started to tear it. He wanted to stop talking and get back to work. "Only two things those guys care about."

"What would they be?" I asked, and I waited.

Duck threw the last of the box on the pile. He was done.

"Money or revenge. In that world, nothing else matters."

CHAPTER TWENTY-NINE

When I got home after my talk with Duck, I was in what my mother would have called a real state. The situation was worse than I had expected, and even more confusing.

I had thought that I had figured everything out, but the facts were different now. It felt like sand slipping out from under my bare feet when the tide pulled the water out. The unknowns, and my fears, were rushing in to fill the hollows. Who did I know who was new to the area and didn't seem to be who they said they were?

There was only one person I could think of.

And he served frozen fish.

I was right. It had to be Kurt.

If George could convince Nolan to look at the photographic gear stowed in the food truck, we might get some answers. In the meantime, all I could do was turn off my brain. There was only one way I knew how to do that: I had to make something. Nothing else would settle me down.

I made my plan. I would walk Toby, cook something simple, and knit socks. I had a pair almost done for my son in Toronto for his birthday. One more good evening, and they would be done. I'd go to the post office in the morning and mail them off. Life would deliver me some answers when it was ready.

Toby and I had a fast walk. Dark clouds were rolling in across the cove. I knew that it wouldn't be long before the sky opened up. I did my best to let Toby have all the smells he needed, but the rain cut us short. We made it back into the house just in time.

It felt good to be home, out of the rain, safe from trouble. The dated decor my aunt had left me was reassuring. The house looked much like it had when I had come here growing up. It was a cocoon of simpler times, of rooms full of people and laughter, of meat-and-potato dinners, and of dishes that were washed by hand before the tea was even made.

I needed to feel some of that world now, some of the predictability and stability that I had grown up with. So, I turned on the kettle, just like my mother and my aunt would have done, and sat down at the Formica kitchen table to plan my dinner.

I looked at the collection of cookbooks I had inherited, on the shelf over the fridge. Most had been published by church groups; all had stains where wooden spoons had been laid to hold open the pages. Next to them was a well-worn copy of Madame Benoit's *Encyclopedia of Canadian Cuisine*, and beside that, the slim volume of wartime recipes Catherine had left for me.[2] I pulled that one out and sat down to read.

---

2. Devonna Edwards, Wartime Recipes from the Maritimes 1939–1945 (Halifax, Nova Scotia: Nimbus Publishing, 2001,), 50, 69, 44.

I turned a page. Near the middle of the book, I found a recipe for a "Six O'Clock Casserole" made of canned spaghetti, cooked peas, and a cup of chicken. A potato "salad" that called for Jell-O and radishes. One recipe even suggested stretching a meatloaf with bananas. But outdoing them all were "Sausage U-boats": baked potatoes filled with boiled and fried sausages, topped with a gravy made from drippings, flour, and water. "Serve at once," the recipe ordered. I imagined that that would be necessary, to catch the family before they ran screaming from the room.

After supper, I settled myself into my comfortable chair with Toby. I was deep into my worries and my knitting when I was interrupted by the sound of my phone ringing. I'd left it plugged in on the counter in the kitchen. I pushed my dog gently out of the way, got up, and made my way over to answer it. I figured the call would be either from Sylvie with a blimp-guy report or from Darlene to update me on the Kosoulas family's takeout-window negotiations.

To my surprise, the call was from Noah.

"I wanted to say 'Congratulations,' Sherlock," he said.

"Sherlock? What are you talking about?" I asked.

"I still have my sources," Noah laughed. "Can't get much past me. I understand you are the one who got George Kosoulas to tip off the RCMP about Kurt."

I leaned against the counter. "What do you mean?"

"The pictures, the digital files." Noah sounded pleased to have a story again, I could tell. "Close-up shots of the Inn, and the people who were there before that woman was killed. There's lots of Rollie and Catherine, but some of Ms.

Coates and Wallace, too. The guy was definitely a stalker, if not something worse."

"Worse?" Slow down, my instincts told me, one step at a time.

"Yup. Your buddy Kurt has been picked up. Nolan has taken him in for questioning—at least, that's the official line. But I wouldn't be surprised if they charged him."

"With what?"

"Murder. The way I see it, he has to be the guy who did it. Killed Rebecca Coates. That makes the most sense. If I am right, you can take it easy, Valerie," Noah said. "Thanks to you and George, I have a feeling it's all over."

CHAPTER THIRTY

I had a moment of peace when I woke up the next morning, then the thoughts rushed in. I remembered the call from Noah. If the RCMP had Kurt in custody and Noah was right, we could all relax. If it turned out that the fake fish-and-chip seller had been sent down by organized crime, the ones Duck's informants were worried about, the RCMP would find that out, too. Dawn was good at her job. But would she be able to get him to tell her why he had been sent?

I was wide awake now. I sat up in bed and pushed Toby over. A dress of Darlene's she wanted shortened was hanging over the back of a chair. It was a fancy one, another wrap she had worn years ago. Lately, she was wearing outfits I hadn't seen on her in a long time. This wardrobe revival, she insisted, had nothing to do with George Kosoulas.

I got out of bed and went over to examine the dress, which, in my opinion, was already short enough. Toby raised his head, looked at me with one eye, then went back to sleep. Darlene had bought this dress in her former life, to wear to a hairstylists' convention in Las Vegas.

Las Vegas. The pulsing, brightly lit oasis in the desert that they could even see from space. I remembered that Darlene had told me that the city had been founded in the middle of nowhere with criminal proceeds by the Mob as a place where anyone from anywhere could kick back and get away from it all. A good investment.

That was it. Duck was right. This wasn't about golf courses, it was about money. Laundered money.

I reached for my phone. I would call Dawn Nolan. She needed to know what questions to ask Kurt. For once, I was way ahead of the RCMP.

"The investigation has moved onto a new level," the familiar voice said, as if she were reading a script. "I have been instructed not to take any more tips from the general public."

"Tips? What are you talking about?" I asked. Honestly, it was time they got this woman out from behind the plexiglass and doing something useful. "I am not the general public. I am the only person who has solid, time-sensitive, information."

"Ha, you wish," the officer said. "This is Gasper's Cove. Anything happens around here, and everyone and their dog calls in with advice. I don't know why this community even needs the RCMP. Everyone's an expert."

"You're not even going to take my message?" I asked.

"Let's make a deal," the officer sighed. "If Officer Nolan comes out here from the back room, where she's doing real work, interrogating a real suspect, and tells me, 'I can't figure it out, we better call Valerie Rankin,' I'll give you a call. How's that sound?"

"Great. I'll wait to hear from her," I said. "Make sure she knows I have something important to tell her." Why did no one take me seriously? "How long do you think it will take for me to hear from her?"

"Can't say," the officer was young, and I heard a be-nice-to-older-women tone in her voice, like she was a visitor at Seaview Manor. "Look, Val, don't you have a life? Aren't you supposed to be doing craft-type things and running a store? Why don't you get back to that? Go about your business."

"Alright," I said. I had finished knitting my socks the night before. "I have to go to the post office. Something important to do there. But I'm going to keep my phone on, remember that."

"Writing the message for Officer Nolan now," the officer said in a voice that made clear that she wasn't. "Have a good one."

I wondered if the clerk at the Canada Post counter was related to the officer at the RCMP desk. Everyone I talked to today was a skeptic.

"I don't know," she said, doom in her voice. "It's going to cost you extra to get it there on time. A whole twenty dollars." She looked over her glasses at me. Why waste that kind of money, she seemed to ask. Was I crazy? "Are you sure it wouldn't be okay if it arrived a day or two later? Twenty dollars," she repeated.

"No. I definitely want to send it," I said. "It has to be there by the twenty-first. It's for a birthday. Hand-knitted socks for my son. I know I should have mailed them earlier, but they took me longer than I expected to finish. The yarn was fine."

"Got it." The woman behind the counter was now sympathetic. "Those four tiny needles, I don't know how you knitters do it. Me, I'm a crocheter. It works up fast." She hesitated. I suspected that she was a mother, too. "But a birthday, you're right, better get it there on time. Express is your best bet."

"Okay, then that's what I'll do. Express." I'd written on the card that I'd put love into every stitch. Too much, I knew, for a mid-twenties son, but it was true. I wanted my boy to read it on the day.

The clerk reached for a small form and began to write, printing carefully in the very small boxes. "Rankin. I know the last name," she chuckled. "First name? Which of the boys is having the birthday?"

"Chester," I said, "But put down C. J. Rankin."

The clerk looked up at me. "What's wrong with Chester?" she asked. "Family name, isn't it?"

"No, it was a name in a book I read once," I explained. "I like it, but he's shortened it. For business reasons, he said." At least, that was what he had told me, although I didn't quite understand why anyone who worked in finance, even in Ontario, couldn't be called Chester.

"Well, we know who he is, even if they don't in the big city," the postal worker winked at me. "Address for delivery?"

I told her.

"Sign here," she said. "Listen, the name, nothing wrong with the name Chester. I've got a better one. My dad's name was Norval."

"That's not one you hear very often," I said diplomatically.

"It's what was on the birth certificate," the clerk said. "It's quite a funny story. My grandfather was a pharmacist, down the coast. Anyway, they named my dad after the man who owned the company that made the drugstore's best seller. And you know what that was?" She waited for my response. I could tell she had delivered the punch line before, many times.

"Can't imagine. What was it?" I asked.

"Feminine products." The postal clerk laughed. The story was better every time she told it. "How's that for a reason to be called Norval?"

"Good as any, I guess. Did your dad mind?" I asked.

"Not really, he was a pharmacist, too, to his bones, right to the day he died at ninety-seven. When his mind started to go, he started counting his cheerios with a knife, you know, by fives."

Somewhere in the back of my mind, muffled behind a thousand competing thoughts, a little alarm went off.

"By fives?" I asked. "Why would he do that?"

The woman behind the counter was surprised at the question. "Because he was a pharmacist. Like they used to count pills in the drugstores," she explained. "In the old days, before the machines. Little trays and a spatula, by fives. It was fast and accurate, my dad said."

The thought at the back of my mind pushed its way to the front of the line and took a seat. I remembered. Why had it taken me so long to figure this out? There were only a few more facts to check, and then I could go in person to the RCMP. This time, they would listen. They had the wrong man.

"Got to go," I said. "I have a call to make. Thanks for the help." I turned and almost ran out of the store. My cell phone was already out of my pocket.

There was only one person who had the information I needed.

Noah.

CHAPTER THIRTY-ONE

"Chill. Take it easy. Those are a lot of questions. I don't understand." I had caught Noah at home, on his way out to catch a good morning wave.

I forced myself to slow down. "That book you're writing, you remember?" I asked.

"Of course I remember. I'm the one writing it," Noah said. "What about it?"

"You can tell me I'm crazy later, just listen. Say the Mob is involved in a development project down here so they can unload money and make it legitimate. Money laundering, right?"

"Yes," Noah was alert. "What about it?"

"The Mob is more than one clan, or family, aren't they?" I continued, ignoring his question while I tried to channel Netflix for the right words, trying to make everything fit what Duck had told me.

"Sure," Noah said. "Where are you going with this?"

"I'm getting there. How about if one branch of organized crime sent someone—say, a Kurt—down here on a project, and they began to think someone else was already here doing the same thing, maybe hiding out or covering up their own stolen cash? I mean, these are suspicious people. They don't trust. What would happen next? Kurt was interested in what the Inn cost, and he took a lot of pictures of the people in it. Why would he do that?" I asked.

"No idea," Noah said. "Are you suggesting that Kurt thought Rollie had funneled illegal cash into buying a bed-and-breakfast so he could quietly live off renting rooms?"

"Exactly," I said. "You're sharp. The way I see it, if you are a criminal, you are going to be predisposed to thinking everyone else is crooked."

Noah started to respond, then a trace of a newshound's curiosity and suspicion passed over his face. "How *did* Rollie afford to buy the Inn, anyway? Wasn't he just some kind of civil servant when he was away?" he asked. "With all that property, the Inn has to be worth a fortune."

"That's probably what Kurt thought. But I know where he got the money. Catherine's father had a lobster license," I said. "She inherited it and sold it."

"That explains things," Noah said. "So, back to my book. What does it have to do with all of this?"

"Everything," I said. "Rollie is no criminal hiding out down here with illegal funds. We know that, even if Kurt doesn't. But that doesn't mean the Mob isn't partly right. What if there is someone else here with a bad past?" I asked. "Those unsolved crimes you told me about got me thinking. I want to know more about them."

"Which one?" Noah asked. "The Great Toonie Heist? That's a good one."

"Yes, that was interesting," I agreed, "but there was another one. Let me think. Someone who didn't show for a train ride? Nothing to do with coins or paintings. Does that ring any bells?"

"Oh, right. The Assiniboine Bandit. That the one you mean?" Noah asked.

"Maybe, can you tell me more about him?"

"Eddy Brown? The veterinary drug rep? That guy? He had a wife who thought he had to travel to farms for work. But guess what? Half the time, he was off robbing banks," Noah said. "You can't make a story like that up."

"Poor woman," I said. Some men were born liars. I knew. "What happened to him? What was the robbery?"

"It was a big gang who did the job," Noah said. "It was some kind of a bank transfer, came into Winnipeg by air. I guess they had someone on the inside who got them a waybill so they could pick up the goods, make it look legit, which, of course, it wasn't. Beal was their usual getaway contact, an ordinary, messy, overweight, harmless-looking guy no one would notice. He was supposed to pick up the shipment, put it in a couple of suitcases, and take it by rail out west. But he didn't show up later at the train station like he was supposed to. Instead, he flew off with the loot."

"What do you mean, 'flew'?" I asked.

"'Flew,' as in a plane. Beal had a small one he used to get in and out of small farming communities," Noah explained. "He wasn't just a drug rep. He was also a pilot."

Maybe he still is, I thought.

I said goodbye to Noah and wished him luck with his book. He seemed concerned that I was fixated on a man the RCMP already had in for questioning.

"I appreciate you want to know what's going down," he said. "You and everyone else. But people who know what they're doing are on it. Don't let yourself get amped up."

"Amped? Me?" I asked, as if I hadn't been told the same thing in forty-nine different ways my whole life. "You know me, just nosy, can't help it. I don't know what I'm talking about."

"Good, glad you get that," Noah relaxed. I was slightly offended at the speed with which he had filed me away, as the plexiglass officer had, as an annoying busybody.

But he was right: I had more than my share of ideas in my head, and they were moving fast. So fast that before I knew it, I was parked in front of the visitor's center in Drummond.

Gail was alone at the front desk when I arrived. She looked harassed.

"A tour bus just left. Seniors. Lovely people, but, man, why do they get them on the road so early? This is a job for a morning person. Which I am not." She refocused on me. "What brings you in this time of day?"

"I have a question for you about Larry Beal. I understand you rent out your cottage to him. Is that true?" I needed to get this stitched down.

"Yes. He came with the property when I bought the place," Gail said. "The previous people called him a model tenant. They were right. He's neat, keeps to himself, and pays his rent on time. Couldn't be better." She eyed me. "What's this about? Your cousin's not going to raise that occupancy tax, is she?"

"No, nothing like that," I said and then hesitated. Gail had told me a lot about her feelings and her life. It was my turn now. "What I saw in that kitchen at the Inn got to me, Rebecca being dead like that. Since then, I've been scared they're not safe out there." I took a deep breath and waited for Gail to tell me I was worried about nothing. She didn't. "I have been trying to figure things out. I've done some digging. I think there's a good chance your tenant, Larry Beal, is really someone called Eddy Brown, a guy who disappeared with a fortune after a robbery years ago. I think he changed his name and has been hiding out here in Gasper's Cove."

Gail, bless her, didn't tell me I was deranged. Noah had already implied that, and once was enough for one day.

"But the guy runs a blimp," she said. "How does that connect?"

"Beal was a pilot." I was ready for the question. "It's a step down, but still in the sky."

"He does pay his rent in cash—that's always suspicious," Gail said. She was on my side again. This was good. "But what made you think he's this robber guy called Brown?"

"Darlene's cat," I explained, "putting the mail over her dish. And an old man running around crouched down in a crisis because he'd spent so much time in a submarine. Some habits are in you so deep, you don't think about them. Larry Beal counted the screws by fives, like pills. Pharmacists, people in the drug business, do that. I think he's been living here pretending to study algae because it's so boring, everyone would leave him alone." This time, when I said the words out loud, they sounded more far-fetched than they had in my head. "Don't you think it could be possible?"

Gail let out a breath. "There was a guy Jimbo and I knew one time. A team captain, traveled around to all the tournaments. It turned out that he had three wives, each in three different cities. Yes, I've heard of things like this. It does happen. But why are you here? Why did you come to me?"

"Think about it," I said. "It makes sense to me and maybe to you. It's a good idea, but we again have no real evidence, nothing solid." I didn't want to admit what I was about to say next, but it was true. "And let's face it, a professional criminal who has stayed ahead of the law for years might have a few tricks that a sewing teacher and bowler"—I corrected myself—"a *professional* bowler might not think about. Particularly if it involves murdering people."

"True. I have zero experience with actually killing people," Gail said, "but you still haven't told me why you are telling me."

"You're his landlord, right? You have a key. If we go into his place, maybe we can find something linking him to his old life. People keep habits; most of us also keep a memento." Gail and I looked at each other. We both thought of the XXL bowling shirt in her office cupboard.

"You know there's rules," Gail reminded me. "A landlord can't go into a tenant's premises without giving due notice." She sounded as if she were reading from a regulation. "But if I have a criminal renting my place, I want to know. How would this work? I could run out with a notice I wanted to go inside and put it somewhere so it looked like it had been there a while, out of the way ..." I liked the way Gail's mind was working. Candlepin was evidently far more strategic than I had given it credit for.

"Can we go out there? And check it out?" I asked her. "What if he's home?" Now that my plan was closer to execution, I felt anxious.

Gail's nerves were steadier. "He won't be. I saw that blimp go up the coast early this morning. Larry will be under it with his remote, reading data. I'll close down for early lunch." She reached under the desk and pulled out a sign for the door. "I'm ready. Let's roll."

Sylvie was right. I would never have found the place Gail rented to Beal if I hadn't had her with me, giving directions. I was sure that if I had been on my own, I would have missed the turn-off to the steep dirt road down to the water or not seen the small cottage at the bottom hidden behind a large boat shed where, presumably, the blimp was stored between flights.

The walk down the road to the cottage was treacherous. Two or three times, I almost slipped on the round beach rocks that had been used as gravel; once or twice, I had to reach out to a tree or to Gail's arm for support. When we finally reached the wooden deck at the cottage's back door, Gail paused and pulled out a pen and a pad of paper with the municipal crest on it.

"The note," she said, scrawling a few lines before ripping off a page from the pad. She looked around, then lifted the leg of a chair on the deck and placed the note under it. "That will work. Wind blew it." She pulled out a key from her pocket and put it in the lock. "That's funny," she said. "It's open. Larry always locks up." Cautiously, she pushed the door open. “Anybody home?” she called out. She stepped over the threshold with me right behind her.

Ahead of us, a familiar figure suddenly appeared in the doorway between the living room and the kitchen, someone I knew, but who this time was not knitting a mitt or quilting a table runner.

“Oh, hi,” Jane from Maine said. “What brings you two to this neck of the woods?”

CHAPTER THIRTY-TWO

"What are *you* doing here, is more like it," I said, then apologized. "Sorry. That was rude." My nerves were ruining my manners. Uneasy, my eyes noted a driftwood lamp, a big-screen TV, a stack of ragged *National Geographics*, and a small table of radio equipment, complete with headset and tiny cameras. It reminded me of the ham radio setup my uncle used to have in his basement. I wondered if Larry Beal was a lonely man like my uncle had been, finding his real friends over the airwaves. What was Jane doing in this remote cottage? I had my own reason for being here, a sneaky one, but what was hers?

"Yes," Gail said, backing me up. "I own this place. I can ask."

"I'm looking for Mr. Beal. The door was open," Jane said. "I represent Kane Chemical. Do you know where he is? We have some serious business to take care of."

"He's out tracking algae," Gail said. "You should have known—the blimp's not here. And what business? Like robbing banks?"

"What are you talking about?" Jane asked. Somewhere above and behind us, at the top of the road down to the cottage, I thought I heard a car door slam.

"Gotcha, haven't I?" Gail raised her chin, watching for a wobble in the Kane Chemical agent's composure. "You don't know who you're dealing with, do you? Too many dollar signs in your eyes to ask any questions."

Jane looked at us calmly and slowly started to gather some documents that were arranged on the coffee table in front of her, next to a pen. Even from a short distance, I recognized them for what they were. The big Xs at the bottom of each page, next to a place for signatures, gave it away.

"Contracts?" I asked, taking another step closer. The logo was clear, and I realized why it looked familiar. I had seen it on an envelope on the seat of Jane's car, on the back of my bottle of shampoo at home, and on the package of over-the-counter antihistamines in my medicine cabinet. Kane Chemical was a household name, the manufacturer of everything from cleaning products to drugs, to fibers, to textiles.

"Yarn!" I said. As soon as I got it, I felt outraged and deceived. "Bob was right, you and Larry are harvesting lichen to make dye!"

"Dye? Yarn?" Jane laughed. "Small towns, small minds."

Beside me, I felt Gail's shoulders lift and her pink-barbelled muscles tense. I was glad we didn't have a bowling ball with us. If we had one, it might be rolling across the floor in the direction of Jane from Maine's feet.

"Dyes aren't worth our time," Jane continued. "We are interested in something far more significant. Do you have any idea of the pharmacological potential of the local species? The report from our lab on the samples Beal sent was impressive. I'm here to get Mr. Beal's signature on a partnership between our company and the foundation." She stopped talking to look at us. "My apologies. You wouldn't know what I am talking about; I tend to talk over people's heads. I'm just saying that it took someone with Beal's background to know what he found."

Gail took a big breath and rolled the last ball of the set. "Does the name 'Eddy Brown' mean anything to you?"

Jane looked blankly at us. I felt Gail stir uncomfortably beside me. "You don't know who we're talking about, do you? Was Val's reporter wrong?"

"No idea. I don't know any Brown," Jane said dismissively. It was the mention of Noah that had her full attention. "A reporter? I'm here on a mission. Beal is a scientist. We've seen his résumé. That's that. No need to talk to the press." She moved toward us, as if clear on what she had to do next. "My bosses aren't the kind who like publicity."

I felt a jolt in my head as if all my ideas and assumptions had skidded into a wall. Holy Moly, what was I going to do now? Jane was the person Duck had talked about, the someone from away who had been sent down to find Beal, probably to get even with him, and to recover the stolen loot.

I had taught a mobster how to quilt.

I turned around slowly, scanning the inside of the cottage for a way to escape if we needed it, which I thought we might. Why had I insisted we come here, to this isolated cottage at the bottom of a steep road? When we came, I had noticed that the big front window looking out onto the dock was a sliding door, like the one at Noah's house. If I turned around, could we get over there, open it, and escape? There was a boat tied up to the dock. I moved closer to Gail. She was older than I was, but much stronger.

Jane took another step in my direction. Slowly and deliberately, she reached into the inside pocket of her poly-cotton windbreaker, never taking her eyes off me.

She was going for a weapon.

I was done.

I tried to prepare myself for the inevitable. Behind me, I would leave a hundred unfinished sewing projects, three children, and a dog. What would Toby do without me? What would happen between Darlene and George? Would Chester like his socks? Would Stuart and I have had a chance? Who would run next month's retreat? Were all three kids going to buy a family place here for the summers?

Would I miss all that? This was too soon. I wasn't ready.

Jane's hand was still in her pocket when her eyes shifted slowly to the glass door behind us. I heard it slide open. I felt the fresh summer air come into the room, sharp with salt, ocean water, and hope. It made me want to cry.

I froze, unable to turn around, transfixed, watching Jane's face watch what was behind me. I heard a heavy thump and the sound of something being dragged, slapping along wooden boards, and then a stumble on the threshold. A voice I recognized.

"Anyone have a knife?"

CHAPTER THIRTY-THREE

Sylvie pushed open the sliding door.

"The rope," she said, "There's too much of it. Larry usually has it cut up and coiled for me, but it's just thrown on the deck. I'll never carry it up to the van unless I cut it into sections. He uses an electric rope cutter, but I don't know where that is." She stepped through the door and into the room, leaving the tangle of old lobster rope out on the deck behind her. She squinted as her eyes adjusted to the dimmer light inside and looked around. "I saw your car up there at the top, Valerie, so I thought I'd poke my head in. Why are you all here?"

"Visiting," I said.

Sylvie nodded, satisfied. Locally, "visiting" was a blanket term used to cover any time a person showed up unannounced. It was always assumed that the visitor had either gossip to share or time to kill. No other explanation was usually offered or given.

"Got it," Sylvie said, looking around for the teapot. Visiting usually involved putting the kettle on.

"We're just wrapping up," Jane said. She pulled a checkbook from her pocket and laid it on the table before looking at me, a question on her face.

I shook my head. What if Jane was right? She'd seen a résumé, I hadn't. "No reporters," I said.

Jane put the checkbook away.

Sylvie looked at us, one to another, mystified. "Am I missing something?" she asked.

"You didn't miss anything," Jane said. "Except a case of mistaken identity, these two being the ones who made the mistake. They thought a scientist was someone else."

Gail rallied, ready to change the subject. "We were having an interesting chat with Jane," she said to Sylvie. "She's here to do some business with Mr. Beal. It turns out craft workshops aren't all she does. Jane also works for Kane Chemicals. Big job, I figure. They're interested in lichen, if you can believe that."

"Big Bob's lichen?" Sylvie asked. She seemed impressed and maybe a little intimidated by Jane's new credentials. "You're not seeing Larry because of his algae?"

"No, just the lichen, for the moment at least." Jane was crisp. I knew fed up when I saw it. It was time we left.

Gail seemed to think the same thing. "I'll check the shed for the rope cutter," she said as she moved to the back door. "Sylvie, we can help you load up."

"You go," Jane said. It was more an order than a reassurance. "I'll stay here and wait. Beal knows we have a meeting." She picked up the contracts and clicked her pen. It felt like a statement of her official capacity and resources. "As to our conversation, it would be premature to disclose what we talked about to anyone else. Actions like that have consequences," she finished, talking like a lawyer. The implication was clear: Talk about the lichen, and lawyers will be involved.

Gail was unfazed. "Whatever," she said. "No one would be interested." She looked at Sylvie as she left. "We can deal with that rope and get out of here."

When Gail returned with the cutter, we plugged it in and used its hot blade to cut through the rope, slicing it into manageable sections. These Sylvie deftly wrapped up, handing one bundle to Gail and one to me to carry, then we headed up the road to her van.

As soon as we moved to the door, Jane turned her back to us and looked out at the water. We had been dismissed.

Outside, when Sylvie was out of earshot, Gail faced me.

"That went well," she said, rearranging the coil of rope in her arms. "So much for your outlaw theory. The guy's a legitimate scientist doing business with a chemical company. That's that. You had me there, I got to admit it. The only good thing is, I am pretty sure old Jane has written us off as a couple of nutcases and will forget everything we said."

"You're right," I agreed. I was down to my last nerve, as my mother would say, and it showed. For a moment, I had thought an employee from a huge company was a hit man. I'd keep that one to myself. "I might have gotten carried away, but I felt something was not right. I have work to do at the store, so I'll try to think this through while I'm there. Darlene is taking care of Toby today."

Gail studied my face. I was surprised to see concern in her eyes. "Are you going to be okay? Maybe you should take a break."

"I will," I said. "Promise. I'm going to be just fine."

It was a relief to be alone in the store. When I arrived, Colleen and Duck were locking up, but I told them not to bother. I'd do it. I stood at the big front window and watched them go. I felt the ancient building sigh with me, wrap its arms around my shoulders, and tell me that it was all going to be okay.

The store should know. My great-great-grandfather had established the business against common sense on this small island on one simple principle: Be where the customers were. To him, those were the families who fished from sailboats. Many of the descendants of those same families still lived here, surviving like the Rankins had through two world wars, the Great Depression, and the decline of the fisheries, transitioning from a general store full of fishing gear to one that sold locally made crafts. Now that I had seen Bob's mitts, I wanted to sell those, too, like I did Sylvie's wreaths. I made my way to the stairs to the second floor to make space when my phone rang.

"Valerie?" I didn't recognize the number, but I knew the voice. "Where are you?"

I stopped on the first step and stood still.

"Here, at the store," I said.

"Great. Would you mind if I dropped by?" Larry spoke softly, but I could hear the excitement in his voice. "You know when you asked me to keep an eye out for anything I saw with the blimp? I have something. You're going to want to see it."

"What did you see? Tell me."

"I can't do it over the phone." Larry sounded rushed. I thought that I heard traffic in the background. He had left the coast and was in his car. "Too hard to explain. I think someone's following me. We need to meet. I am not sure, but I think what I saw involves Rollie. Not good. We can't waste time."

Rollie? He had me.

"Okay," I said. "I'll be at the front door. Front Street. Waiting for you."

CHAPTER THIRTY-FOUR

Larry arrived in minutes. He must have been on the causeway when he called. Instead of stopping in front of the store at the empty curb, he swung around and crossed over to the small lot behind the boat shed next to the wharf. He parked there between two trucks and then jogged across the street to meet me.

I held the door open for him.

"Sorry to bother you, but this seemed the best thing to do," Larry said. Now that he was in front of me, the nervousness had gone, replaced by a calm assurance I had not seen in him before. "I hope I'm not interrupting anything."

"No, just me. I came in to rearrange some things upstairs in the Co-op."

"That place where you sell crafts?" Given the urgency of his phone call, I was surprised Larry was making small talk. "I've never seen it. Can I come up and have a look?"

"Of course," I said, trying to speed this up. "Follow me. I want to hear what you found."

"You will," Larry said, closing the door behind him. "Right behind you."

Halfway up the stairs to the Co-op, I stopped.

"Aren't you supposed to be meeting Jane from Maine and signing some chemical contracts?" I asked. I hadn't had time to think of this before, but it came to me now. "For our lichen that doesn't belong to you. Big Bob was right—someone was starting to harvest it from the trees. It was you, wasn't it?"

I felt a hand on my back. Larry leaned in closer to me and whispered in my ear, even though we were alone. "Keep walking." I caught the smell of whisky on his breath. Local men drank rum. "You think you're awful smart, don't you? But not smart enough."

We were at the top of the stairs when I turned around. This was my safe place, where I came to connect to myself and what mattered in my life. It didn't feel so safe now.

"What do you mean?" I asked.

Larry reached over and turned the volume dial on the old sound system up. To mask sounds, I realized. I felt sick.

"That deal with Kane was my fee for finding them a gold mine," he said, raising his voice. "That's going public soon anyway. But that's not why I'm here."

"Then, why are you? You don't have anything to show me, do you?" I looked around for a way to protect myself from this man if I had to. Quilted oven mitts? Hand-carved wooden spurtles, the kind they used to stir oatmeal?

"I had to get in the door." Larry was matter-of-fact. "Who are you? How do you know? I heard it all. Didn't you see the spy cams at my place? Sloppy."

Startled, I remembered the ham-radio setup in Gail's rental. It had never occurred to me that those little cameras had been turned on.

"You have your place bugged?" I wasn't sure if "bugged" was the right word, but it was all I could think of. "Why?"

Larry almost smiled. "It's part of my own personal witness-protection program."

"Excuse me?"

"I'm trying to protect myself from witnesses. Why else would I be living here in the middle of nowhere? Now, tell me who you are and who you are working for." Larry ran his hands over a quilt on a rack, taking his time.

"I'm exactly who I say I am," I said. I was trapped, and I knew it, and that made me reckless. "Which is more than I can say for you, Eddy Brown."

At the sound of his name, one he hadn't used for so long, Larry's face hardened. "I knew I should have moved faster. She got the word out."

"She?" I ran through all the shes I could think of, but I knew there was only one he meant. "Rebecca Coates? What did she ever do to you?"

"It's what she could have done. What are the odds?" Beal asked. "A reporter who covered the story in Manitoba showing up here? I was in town, getting supplies, and I passed her on the street. It took her a minute, but I think she recognized me. I had to get her out of town before she put two and two together."

"But why sabotage the Inn?"

"She was staying there. I was on the coast and slipped in. I'd been meaning to do something about the Inn for a while. I've got a deal cooking with a chemical company. The last thing I need is a bunch of tourists crashing around the woods. Before the Inn, I had my solitude. But when I saw her again, I figured I'd do two birds with one stone. I wanted to work with the propane in the kitchen, burn the place down, but I ran out of time. The dishwasher was fast and easy. I got lucky that she was the one to touch it." Larry stopped smiling when he noticed me. "You should tell your cousin Rollie to lock his doors at night."

"I will," I said. "As soon as I get home." I swallowed. "I'm going home, right?"

"What do you think?" Larry sighed. "Rebecca's dead because she knew who I was. And, it turns out, so do you." He hesitated. "Unless you told someone else? What about this reporter you talked about?"

"I didn't say anything to anyone," I said quickly, but in case he knew something about women like me and knew that was unlikely, I added, "I wasn't going to say anything until I was sure. And the reporter is only someone writing a book about old crimes. He knows the name but not that you're here. That part, I figured out. It was the cat dish that did it. That and the way you counted screws. Like a pharmacist."

"Cat? Geez, no one's going to miss you." He reached over, grabbed my shoulders, and pushed me against the wall, next to the big window that faced the water. He reached over and started to crank the pane of the little window on the side open. "Quite a drop," he said. "Tall old building."

I looked past him and saw the white caps on the waves. I'd heard something in Beal's voice, and I recognized it for what it was.

"You're afraid, aren't you?" I asked. "And you have been for a long time." That's why he was here. Despite his brains and his training, with all that money, he had traded it all away and paid for it with his peace. He'd spent his time in hiding, watching for enemies, waiting to be discovered, afraid someone would come and get him, not knowing who they were.

"Everybody's afraid," he said. "You can't tell me that right now you aren't, and most of every day."

"You know what?" I said. "I'm not." As soon as I said it, I knew that it was true. Here, where I lived, I was secure. There wasn't a street in Gasper's Cove where I didn't feel safe, where I wouldn't feel comfortable knocking on any door and asking for help. I trusted everyone around me, and I knew that they felt the same way about me. The people in this community had taken care of each other before I was born. I knew that they would do the same for anyone I left behind when I was gone. This thought made me feel calm, even now, with Beal ready to do to me what he'd done to Rebecca Coates.

"They'll find you," Beal continued. He wanted to sound confident, but again, I heard the fear behind the bravado in his voice. "They'll never find me. I'll disappear again. I'm getting good at it."

The window was fully open now. The smell of salt blew in. Beal moved close to me.

I decided that the last thing I wanted was the last word.

"You can try," I said. "But I have a piece of advice for you from an old sewing teacher. Next new identity you try? Don't try to take your old clothes with you. You used to be a big man, Mr. Beal. That fit of your collar on your new skinny neck? Dead giveaway."

CHAPTER THIRTY-FIVE

"What?" For a moment Beal hesitated, distracted. This was all I needed. I knew the layout of the Co-op in my sleep. I slipped my left hand behind me. Reaching back into the basket of locally made Nova Scotia sea-kelp skin-care products, I found what I needed. I gave it my best shot.

Right between the eyes.

There was blood everywhere. Beal grabbed his face, and I wondered if I had broken his nose. I hoped so. It was the least I could do.

A dog barked.

Toby. The big dog tore up the stairs, Darlene and Sylvie behind him. With a brief look to me for permission, my beautiful golden lunged forward, knocking the Assiniboine Bandit to the ground and pinning him there.

"What's going on?" Darlene shouted. She and Sylvie stood at the top of the stairs, their arms loaded with new wreaths.

"Our friend Larry Beal isn't only an algae man," I said. I started to shake and sat down. "His real name is Eddy Brown, the flying pharmacist, part of a gang he stole from.

He came down here to hide." Beal tried to move, and Toby growled, deep in his throat.

"Get out!" Sylvie squeaked. "But why is he covered in blood? And why's Toby standing on his chest?"

"Because he's a killer. Toby knows. Beal killed Rebecca Coates. It was about her all along. She used to be a reporter. He thought she recognized him." I reached into the skin-care basket for another weapon if I needed it.

Sylvie watched me. "Is that one of my bath bombs?" she asked. "Did they ever sell?"

"Not really," I admitted. "They don't really dissolve, but they do have their uses."

"I can see that," she said. "But one question. If Larry here"—she motioned to the bleeding criminal lying on the floor in front of my cash counter—"really is who you say he is, how did you figure it out?"

"The mail on your cat's dish, Darlene. The things you do but don't remember why you do them." Both Sylvie and Darlene looked confused, so I kept going. "The screws I dropped on the floor. Mister here"—I tapped Beal's foot with mine—"counted them in fives. That's how pharmacists used to count pills, on little trays with a spatula." Beal groaned. I hoped that he was uncomfortable. "You know, Noah's writing a book. That's when I found out the Assiniboine Bandit worked with veterinary drugs. That he flew into rural communities. It was obvious."

"You mean the blimp?" Sylvie said. "It makes sense." She had always been an excellent lateral thinker.

Darlene was more practical. "What do you want us to do now?" she asked.

"Calling 911 would be a good idea," I said. Beal opened one eye. I held another of Sylvie's weapons above my head, and he shut it again. "We should tie him up."

Sylvie smiled. "Not a problem," she said, laying her wreaths on the counter. "I'm good with rope."

Sylvie did a wonderful job, although it took both Darlene and me to get Toby off Beal's chest so she could work. When Officer Nolan and the rest of the RCMP arrived, they were impressed. Sylvia had Beal trussed up like a turkey, with ropes woven around him in knots that had to be cut because they could not be untied.

"Almost decorative," one of the officers noted, which made Sylvie beam. "How much are your wreaths?"

"Fifty dollars," Sylvie answered. "Although you'll get the friends and family discount."

"Put two away for me," the officer said.

Nolan rolled her eyes. "Paramedics say he'll be okay, but what did you hit him with?" she asked. "You did some damage."

"A bomb," I said.

"A bomb?" Nolan's eyes went wide.

"Bath bomb. One of mine," Sylvie chipped in. "May have overdone the salt. Or the kelp."

"I see," Nolan said, backing away from us, making way for the paramedics. "I'll watch myself with you two."

Sylvie and I took that as a compliment.

A few days later, Darlene and I met for lunch at the Agapi. Darlene was catching me up on the talk she and George had had at the look-off when Dawn Nolan walked into the restaurant. She stopped by our table.

"Can I have a word with you?" she asked.

"Of course." I picked up a menu and tapped a new item at the top listed under *Appetizers*. "The Darlene platter?" I read, stopping to raise an eyebrow at my cousin. "Marinated feta, tzatziki, skordalia, taramasalata, pita, and dolmades? Guaranteed to satisfy?" I put the menu down. "You gotta be kidding. What is this? A Greek restaurant guy engagement ring?"

"Oh, stop it," Darlene said, pleased to be discussing this. "One step at a time. Not everyone gets a chance to try again. We're not going to waste it."

I loved a good ending.

We both sat there in silence for a moment, enjoying that this was exactly what Darlene had.

"I should go talk to Dawn," I said to my cousin, "but before I go, I want to thank you. The way you and Toby showed up that night."

"Strange, wasn't it?" Darlene asked. "I was taking Toby back down to your place, but he wanted to walk down the hill to the store. It was like he knew you needed him."

"I think he did," I said. Nolan caught my eye. "Keep me posted. I have some unfinished business I need to take care of."

"You go," Darlene said, smiling as George brought her another baklava. "I'm already taken care of."

I moved to Dawn Nolan's table and sat down.

She got right to the point. "We received a message from Halifax," she said. "The Bedford Institute of Oceanography had been in touch with a pharmaceutical company. They had samples of Nova Scotia lichen provided by a private operator. The company had plans to get that person to sign a release so they could set up a formal agreement to harvest. B.I.O. wanted us to check them out. That was when a certain algae blimp got on our radar."

"The person representing that company was Jane from Maine," I said. "She told us. And that private operator was Larry Beal?"

"Exactly," Nolan said. "I have to say, good call figuring out his real name. I give you that. But you were close to getting into real trouble. Do you know that?"

"Better than anyone. I was the one who had to hit him with the bomb, wasn't I?" I felt that the RCMP should be more appreciative. "But when did you know who he was?"

"As soon as Noah contacted us. Your visit to him got him thinking, and since he has more sense than you do, he came to us." Nolan was serious. I felt like I was in the principal's office, getting a lecture. "Once we had a name, it came together. It turns out in his other life, Beal had been quite a talented chemist, top of his class at the University of Manitoba, but frustrated with his job. And he was greedy—they always are."

"He stole from the gang and came here," I finished. It was a lot to take in. "But what about Kurt? He was watching the Inn. Why? What's the connection?"

"Kurt Gordon?" Nolan laughed. "Now that's a character with a past. Failed golf pro, ex-military police, lightweight private investigator from Woodstock, Ontario. He won't say, but I think some of the boys hired him to come down and see if Beal was here." Nolan took a sip of her Greek coffee and grimaced. The Kosoulas version was strong and an acquired taste. "As smart as Beal was, you know what tipped them off?"

I shook my head.

"A bus tour of the Maritimes. Some connected guy's dad came down here and brought back some pictures of the beach. Beal was in it with the blimp, small and blurry, but the son thought he recognized him."

I had a sudden image of Brown/Beal's face, all the anxiety he lived with, running his own personal witness-protection program. Sometimes, it is the ones you can't see, like seniors on a bus, who will get you.

"But the Inn?" I asked. "Why was Kurt watching it?"

"Because he didn't know what he was doing," Nolan said. "No real investigative skills whatsoever. But he had to come up with something for his clients. He looked around for someone who had the cash to make a large purchase out of nowhere."

"Right idea, wrong person," I said. "Is that where the foundation came in?"

"You got it. The foundation was a front, something Beal made up himself. It's a registered charity, and those don't have to reveal the source of donations. It's an old money-laundering loophole we're trying to change. He had to have a way to quietly dispose of his income."

"In the most boring way possible," I said. "And the algae gave him a reason to be here and a reason to be left alone." I had another thought. "But the algae was connected to the lichen. Bob told me they grow together. It was the lichen he was really mapping, wasn't it?'

"Right again," Nolan admitted. "But once again, being clever wasn't enough for him. He could have lived here quietly, but once an operator, always an operator, I guess," Nolan said. "Under pressure, you default to who you are."

I nodded, remembering an old man at a summer camp, running crouched down into a fire. "But Bob picked it up, didn't he?" I asked. "He realized someone was harvesting the lichen, stripping the trees."

"Yes, he did," Nolan said. "He finally came to me, convinced something was up. To be honest, any other officer wouldn't have listened to him, but I know better." She smiled and then tried to hide it. "There's a lot more to Bob than most people realize."

This, I thought, is true of most of us.

"So, what happens now?" I asked.

"Brown, or Beal, is facing charges of theft, fraud, and murder," Nolan said. "Hard to say what that's going to look like, but I'd say the blimp, like its owner, is permanently grounded."

CHAPTER THIRTY-SIX

I was standing on the sidewalk in front of the Agapi, on my way back to the store, when a big black Lexus pulled up beside me. The driver parked and stepped out of the car.

At first, I didn't recognize her. The black linen had been replaced by a flowered pink skirt and a knit top.

"I wanted to say goodbye before I go," Laura Sanders said. "And thank you."

"Thank me? For what? You came here for a quiet retreat, and you ended up in the middle of a murder investigation and a quilting class you had to teach yourself." I paused, still embarrassed. "You got the check, the refund, didn't you? There was nothing I could teach you. I left it at the front desk with Catherine."

"I tore it up," Laura said. "I owe you, if anything."

"You do? Why?"

"That day I spent out there surrounded by water, waiting for the tide to go out, it seemed to me that this was what I was doing with my whole life. Waiting, helpless," she said. "I came here a woman with a man who didn't need her, with no purpose to her life." I didn't say anything. It must have cost her to say that. "Now, I am leaving a woman who doesn't need that fiancé and knows who she is."

I understood this story, but now was not the time to interrupt. "And who do you feel you are?"

"A teacher. A quilting teacher. I was good at the workshop, I know I was. I thought I had nothing anyone needed." She raised a hand to brush some untamed curls out of her eyes. I noticed the rings were gone. "It's how I was raised, I guess. If you did enough for other people, they would appreciate you more. But it doesn't work like that. It just turns your whole life into an endless list of obligations. Being that person, and unnoticed, was exhausting me. That's why I came down here to escape. But you know what you taught me?"

"No." It certainly wasn't how to quilt, I thought.

"When I saw how people lived down here, I realized you shouldn't need a retreat from your own life. I looked at you and the other crafters, at Sylvia and her wreaths, and Bob and his mitts, and it was clear to me. Making things, even in a world when there is so much to buy, isn't a time waster. It is a lifesaver."

I couldn't have said it better myself. "So, what are you going to do?" I asked her.

"Go home. The owner of the local quilt shop is retiring. I'm going to have a chat with her about taking over the business."

"And Parker?"

"He'll have to organize his own life. He has his business, his golf, he'll fish. He asked me what I thought about buying a place down here to get away to. I told him it will depend on my business, and the view." I could see she was enjoying herself. "We'll see. He made some promises. I didn't."

And it was a good view. Stuart and I had driven up to the look-off with Toby and let him run down to the beach on the stone path. As we followed the dog, Stuart reached out and took my hand so I didn't slip and didn't let go.

"You've got to be careful," he said. "The way they've put down these rocks isn't up to code."

"It's been like this since we were kids," I told him. "Our parents didn't want us to play down here, but of course, we did. They were worried we'd fall into one of the old gun platforms and break our necks."

Stuart stopped and looked at me. "Gun platforms? That sounds pretty dramatic."

"I'm not kidding," I said. "They're all along the Atlantic Coast. The navy built them into the cliffs during the war. Little rooms with slits in the hill facing the ocean. They put a couple of guys in there to watch for U-boats. I wonder how much they saw."

"It sounds pretty high stress to me," Stuart said.

"Nah. Some of the old guys said it was five years of watching seagulls. There were a lot fewer of those submarines out there than everyone thought."

"Well, at least they had the water to watch," Stuart said. "I don't need to meditate. I just look at the ocean."

"That's what all the tourists say, too. It's one reason I'm going to be able to run my retreats in the summer. I've already had inquiries about next year."

Toby bounded up the path to meet us. He had a stick in his mouth. Stuart took it and threw it far away.

"I wouldn't let yourself get too booked up," Stuart said, watching the dog. I couldn't see the expression on his face, but I felt him smile. "I didn't want to say anything. You've been known to get worked up." He turned to me now, and, yes, he was smiling. "But your kids have been in touch with me, had me going out and checking on some properties for them. They wanted to surprise you, but I'm telling you before you get too committed. I think they're going to do it. I talked to Gail at bowling; she is going on tour and decided to sell her cottage. I knew the kids wanted to have a place they can come back to in the summers. I contacted them. They're going for it. How do you feel about that?"

I went over to a large rock and sat down. I brushed it off to make room for Stuart to sit next to me. It was covered in lichen. I looked out at the ocean and remembered my ancestors who had escaped the Highland Clearances to come here. I thought of how they had held on and settled, attaching themselves to this coast, building a life to outlast them. Family was all they cared about. And now mine could come home. Part of the year didn't matter. They'd be here. The ties would hold.

"But the money," I said. "They're young. How can they swing it?"

Stuart put both of his hands around mine. "Don't worry. That's taken care of. You just look forward to next summer. That's all you have to do."

I looked at him now, a sailor and a builder. "You made it happen, didn't you? That's a big thing. Why?"

"It's what I wanted," Stuart said. "I knew how much it would mean to you, that's all."

The wind blew my hair in front of my face. Stuart reached over and carefully brushed it out of my eyes. "I'm not going anywhere," he said. "None of us are."

THE END

FURTHER READING

The more I write about Gasper's Cove, the more aware I am of the eccentricity of where I live. My best story ideas come from casual conversations with my neighbors, and they usually send me off looking for more information. The references listed below were those that helped me develop this story. I am sharing them with you in case you might like to know more about any of these subjects and to document that if something I write seems implausible, this being Nova Scotia, it is probably true.

The Algae Mapping Blimp

Years ago one of my students had a boyfriend who ran a research mapping blimp. In a non-criminal way, he is the inspiration for Larry Beal. You can read about the project at

dal.ca/news/2008/07/18/balloon.html

Nova Scotia Lichen

Retired librarian Frances Anderson is a local lichen legend. Gasper's Cove is full of enthusiasts, I think she would fit right in! You can hear her interviewed at

sharedground.captivate.fm/episode/amazing-lichens-with-frances-anderson

U-Boats Off the Nova Scotia Coast

Michael L. Hadley, *U-Boats Against Canada: German Submarines in Canadian Waters* (Montreal, Quebec: McGill-Queen's University Press, 1985)

War-Time Recipes

Devonna Edwards, *Wartime Recipes from the Maritimes 1939–1945* (Halifax, Nova Scotia: Nimbus Publishing, 2001)

READER'S GUIDE

Crafting a Getaway

BY BARBARA EMODI

1. In some ways, this book is about trying to outrun fear. The communities along the north-eastern coast of North America worried about unseen U-boats. Larry Beal feared that the mob would find him. What is Valerie Rankin most afraid of and how does she handle that fear?
2. Officer Dawn Nolan notes that "Fear makes things real, even if they aren't there." Do you agree with her statement? Can you think of an example?
3. The book has a subtheme about finding love later in life. Rollie and Catherine have maybe done it and the ladies of Seaview Manor and Sophia Kosoulas think this is still possible for Darlene and George. Sophia and Bernadette's meddling seems promising. Is setting up couples a good idea? What obstacles do you think might occur before they can truly reconnect?
4. The role of women, of housewives and mothers, managing families on their own during WWII has largely been unwritten. Valerie gets a glimpse of it when she reads the old cookbook. Do you have any stories from your own family of how women of that generation managed life in those times?

5. There is a rivalry between Drummond and Gasper's Cove. Is it real or just in the minds of the residents of Gasper's Cove? If you think the tension is real, why do you feel that it is real, and what feeds it? Are rivalries a positive or a negative?

6. The flavor of Gasper's Cover stems from the obstacles the residents and their ancestors have overcome, from the Highland Clearances and WWII to the decline of the fisheries. How have the experiences shaped the community? Are there similar influences in your community?

7. Throughout the book, there are references to research being done on Nova Scotia algae and lichen. To the author these species are a reminder that the overlooked details of life deserve attention, something she sees in communities like Gasper's Cove. Are there any endangered species of plant or animal you want most to see protected?

8. As soon as Val realizes the scheduling mishap, she calls Darlene. Is there someone you know that always brings calm or takes you closer to a solution?

9. A few times in this novel Val compares herself to Stuart. "I looked down at the watering can on the ground beside my chair. It was brass, with a long, elegant spout like a crane. The one I had at home was green plastic, with a big crack in it because I'd left it out all winter in the snow." In her comparisons, she seems chaotic and disorganized but sees Stuart as steady and methodical. Do you feel this is true? If so, does it bode well or badly for their future?

10. Was there a moment in the book when a character did something that really surprised you?

11. Throughout the story there are examples of behavior done by rote: a cat covering her food dish, counting screws by fives, and crouching down to enter a room in an emergency. Do you know anyone who does something in a certain way even though it may no longer be necessary?
12. A local postal worker shares a humorous story of the origin of a family name. Believe it or not, that is a true story! Does anyone in your family have a unique name origin story?
13. There are three traditional crafts taught in Valerie's workshop, quilting, rope weaving, and knitting thrummed mittens. If you could suggest other topics that might interest summer visitors what would those be?
14. What character in these stories reminds you of someone you know? Why is that?
15. Stuart and Valerie seem to have an ongoing almost romance. Who do you think will make the first move and how will it happen?
16. If there is one line in this book you will remember, what is it?
17. In the end, Laura Sanders notes "I came here a woman with a man who didn't need her, with no purpose to her life. Now, I am leaving a woman who doesn't need that fiancé and knows who she is." Do you think she'll be successful? Is such a large change truly possible?

ABOUT THE AUTHOR

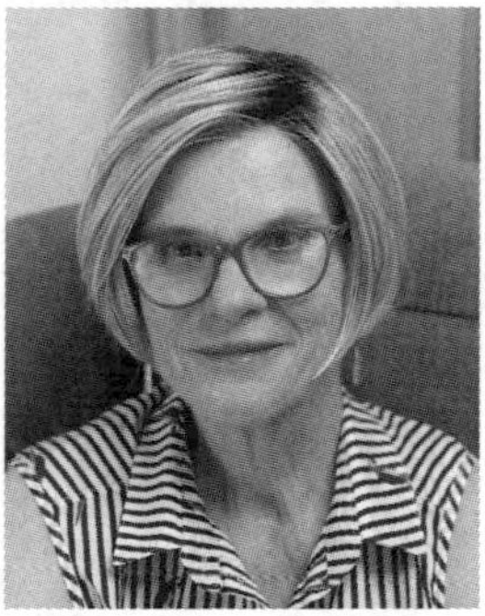

Barbara Emodi lives and writes in Halifax, Nova Scotia, Canada, with her husband, a rescue dog, and a cat, who all appear in her writing in various disguises. She has grown children and grandchildren in various locations and, as a result, divides her time between Halifax; Austin, Texas; and Berkeley, California, so no one misses her too much.

Barbara has published two sewing books—*SEW: The Garment-Making Book of Knowledge*, and *Stress-Free Sewing Solutions*, and she is a course instructor on the innovative and interactive platform Creative Spark Online Learning (by C&T Publishing). In another life, she has been a journalist, a professor, and a radio commentator.

Visit Barbara online and follow on social media!

Website: babsemodi.com
Blog: sewingontheedge.blogspot.com
Instagram: @bemodi
TikTok: @babsemodi
Fiction website: babsemodi.com/blog-posts
Creative Spark: creativespark.ctpub.com

Gasper's Cove Mysteries Series

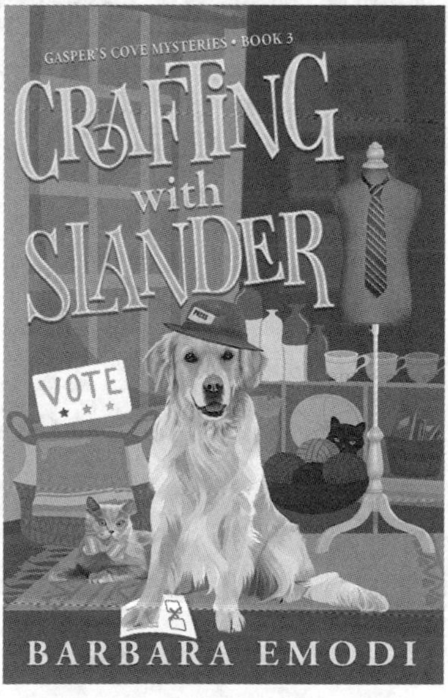

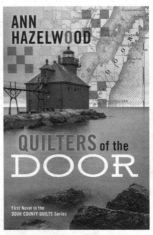